DISNEYLAND HOSTAGE

The Tom and Liz Austen Mysteries
by Eric Wilson

Also available by Eric Wilson
Summer of Discovery
The Unmasking of 'Ksan

DISNEYLAND HOSTAGE

Eric Wilson

A Totem Book
Toronto

First published in 1982 by
Clarke, Irwin & Company Limited.

This edition published in 1983
by TOTEM BOOKS
a division of Collins Publishers,
100 Lesmill Road, Don Mills, Ontario.

Canadian Cataloguing in Publication Data

Wilson, Eric.
Disneyland hostage

ISBN 0-00-222637-5

I. Title.

PS8595.I58D57   1983   jC813'.54   C83-098773-8
PZ7.W55Di   1983

Printed in Canada

I dedicate this book with love
to my bride
Elizabeth Welch Wilson

1

Have you ever been in a plane that's about to crash?

Pulling my seat belt tighter, I read the airline's safety instructions one more time. Then I wiped my sweating palms and looked out the window at the people standing around, totally relaxed.

The plane hadn't even left the ground, and I was already prepared to meet my doom.

The woman in the next seat squeezed my hand. "Just relax, Liz. Don't you love the colour scheme inside this plane?"

That's my Aunt Melody for you. Always seeing the good side while others look for the grim angles. Like the notice that said USE SEAT CUSHION FOR FLOTATION.

"You know what that means, Aunt Melody? When the plane crashes in the Pacific, we'll have to swim for shore holding the seat cushion. I bet old Jaws is already sharpening his teeth, waiting for us to drop in for dinner."

Aunt Melody laughed. "We won't be flying over the Pacific, Liz."

"Sure we will, when they have to dump the fuel before our emergency landing."

"Calm down, Liz. You've flown before."

"I know, but I still hate it. Why can't we get off this death trap and take the train?"

"After what happened to Tom on *The Canadian*, I'm surprised you think trains aren't dangerous."

There's no way I can win an argument with her, so I just sat back and listened to the sweat splash from my forehead. Beside me Aunt Melody calmly returned to reading *Variety*, which is the bible of people in show biz. Not that she's a star, or even on the tube, but she does sing with an opera company in Minneapolis. She'll never be a Big Name, she says, but using her voice makes her really happy and I think that's great.

After inviting me to Minneapolis to visit her and see a performance, she was now treating me to a holiday at Disneyland. The thought of being in California had been giving me goosebumps, I was so excited, but at the moment I could only think of surviving Flight 101 from Minneapolis to Los Angeles.

Suddenly, it began.

There was a dull thump as the big door swung closed, followed by a terrible whistling roar as the engines revved up. *I'm too young to die!* I kept thinking.

The flight attendants enjoyed some kind of sick joke by demonstrating the use of emergency oxygen masks, then the plane was hurtling down the runway. With an amazing thrust of power we angled straight up into the sky, and for a minute I thought the other passengers would come tumbling back toward me. But after a few heart-pounding minutes the plane levelled off.

"Thank goodness that's over!" I exclaimed.

"That's right. Now there's only the landing left."

"Thanks a lot. I'd completely forgotten."

Way below I could see tiny farm houses and the sparkle of miniature lakes and toy cars on a six-lane sliver of road. As I stared at them a hand touched my arm.

I turned and looked up at a hunk of *perfect* man, a vision of golden hair, deep blue eyes, and a gold chain over the hairy chest visible through his open-neck shirt. It took me a few seconds to realize he was speaking to me.

"Pardon?" I stammered. "What did you say?"

"Aren't you Lisa Hewitt, from Richmond?"

"No," I admitted, wishing desperately that I was. "My name is Liz Austen, and I'm from Winnipeg." He looked puzzled, and I added stupidly, "That's in Canada."

"Yes, I know." He shook his golden head. "The next time I see Lisa, I'll tell her she's got a double! You've got the same pretty dark hair and eyes."

He was turning away when Aunt Melody saved the day. "Won't you sit down?" she said, glancing at the empty seat beside her. "We'd enjoy talking to you."

The Vision settled down, and I had a chance to look him over more carefully. There were a couple of tiny scars near his right eye, but nobody's perfect, and I couldn't believe our luck. I was trying to think of a good conversational opening when Aunt Melody jumped right in.

"I don't believe we've had the honour . . . ?"

"What?" the Vision said.

"We haven't been introduced. My name is Melody Symons."

"And I'm Kingsley Fortune. I can tell you're from Canada, Ms. Symons, because you've got such a nice turn of phrase."

"Why, thank you. Please call me Melody."

"Call me Liz," I added. "Have . . ."

But Aunt Melody cut me off with her own question, and I

was left with my jaw flapping. It took me a few moments to stop seeing green, but then I admitted to myself that Kingsley was perhaps a shade too old for me. And if Aunt Melody could somehow make an impression, then maybe we'd see something of him in Los Angeles. What a thought!

Trying to give Aunt Melody some help, I broke into their conversation. "My aunt's been all over the world, Kingsley, and now she's an opera star."

He looked pretty impressed, but Aunt Melody raised her hand. "Not a star at all. Just one of the toilers in the trenches."

Kingsley laughed. "I'll bet you're a beautiful singer."

"Oh, she is! You should get her address in Minneapolis and arrange to go to a performance." I was about to suggest dinner after the show when Aunt Melody gave me a dirty look.

"Why don't you read your book, Elizabeth?" She only uses my full name when she's *furious*. "I'm sure Mr. Fortune doesn't need your help organizing his life."

The Vision smiled at Aunt Melody. "Please, call me Kingsley."

I could swear I heard the fluttering of her gorgeous eyelashes as they fell into conversation. I did a quick study of Aunt Melody, and found everything in perfect order. The huge dark eyes, just the right touch of make-up, a white silk blouse combined with forest-green slacks, and a couple of silver bracelets — she looked like a model.

A flight attendant came around with free soft drinks and some peanuts. "We'll be serving dinner soon," she said, and right away I heard the tension in her voice.

"What's wrong?"

Her smile was so forced it was lopsided. "Everything's fine. Why do you ask?"

"You sound tense. Is something wrong with the plane?"

She studied my eyes, and was just about to speak when Aunt Melody cut in. "Pay no attention to my niece. Flying makes her nervous."

The attendant nodded and walked away. I pretended to be opening the package of peanuts, but I saw her whisper to another attendant who looked my way. Something was wrong for sure, but what could I do? I couldn't get off at the next stop, and I didn't think I could face a parachute even if my life depended on it. *Which it did.* Now I was really sweating, and I quickly got out the key ring my brother Tom gave me. It features both a rabbit's foot and a four-leaf clover.

Kingsley's deep voice interrupted my grim thoughts. "Look at that key ring! I guess you're a superstitious girl, Liz."

"Who, me? No way."

Aunt Melody laughed. "Come on, Liz. Tell the truth."

"Okay, I confess that flying terrifies me. What if there's a bomb in someone's luggage, ticking towards zero hour? What if a bolt on one of those jet engines works loose? In a few minutes the engine might fall off, and then we'll plunge to earth, spinning and twisting, our mouths screaming, our ..."

"Stop!" Kingsley said with a laugh. "Now you've got *me* terrified. You'd better give that rabbit's foot another stroke."

Aunt Melody smiled at him. "Don't encourage her, Kingsley."

"Well, I confess I'm a bit that way myself. That's probably why I noticed that the crew had carefully crossed the seat belts before we came on board, so we may get to L.A. safely."

"I've never heard that superstition before. Got any more?"

"*Macbeth* is considered the unluckiest play by actors, because of the Witches' Song, and we always say 'break a leg' to each other on opening night. We never say 'good luck,' even though that's what we mean."

"You're an actor?"

He smiled, and dimples appeared on his cheeks. "That's right."

"Are you a *star*?"

His smile turned into a wonderful laugh. "You could say so."

"What do you mean?"

"Well, I've just been on location near Minneapolis with the film director Lomas Shaw. I'm sure you've heard of him?"

I hadn't, but I made a gesture that could have been yes or no. Kingsley didn't seem to notice.

"The film's going to be very big, and my agent has several more deals brewing in Hollywood. That's why I'm rushing back to L.A."

"Have you always been an actor?"

"All my life. It's the only work for me."

I studied Kingsley's blue eyes, and his skin that really was "bronzed" from the California sun. I was dying to ask for an autograph but Aunt Melody would have called that gauche. As I checked his hand to make sure he wasn't wearing a wedding ring, I noticed that he had thick callouses, the kind people get from tough labouring. Kingsley saw me staring and stood up.

"Excuse me," he said, and walked away.

I leaned close to Aunt Melody. "Are you making progress?"

"Elizabeth, please."

"Did you notice his hands?"

"Yes. I wonder how an actor gets those kinds of callouses. Kingsley may not be what he claims."

A man of mystery! For a moment I wondered if I could figure out Kingsley's secret, then my good mood collapsed. "If he isn't really an actor in L.A., we may never see him again!"

Aunt Melody laughed. "Would that be a tragedy?"

"He's nice," I said mournfully. "I wouldn't mind hanging around Hollywood with someone as gorgeous as Kingsley. Let's pretend his hands aren't a mystery."

Speaking of hands, the flight attendant had a real tremble in hers as she gave me a tray of food. Something was definitely wrong with the plane, but what could I do? I unwrapped the cutlery from a paper napkin and studied the tray.

The whole meal was in front of me, including two desserts:

fudge and cookies. I ate a couple of cookies, then gobbled a black olive from a watery-looking salad. The beef was only okay, so I decided to finish off the cookies and fudge.

The plane angled, and I looked out at the sunshine. Then it angled further and I was in the shade of the wing with rays of yellow light splashing past on both sides. At this peaceful moment, the pilot came on with a terrible announcement.

"We have a problem in our hydraulic gear," she said, and then paused, knowing the passengers would start babbling. That's exactly what happened. One guy was even swearing, but a flight attendant got him calmed down. Meanwhile I just grabbed Aunt Melody's hand and squeezed my rabbit's foot as tightly as I could. My heart was pounding something awful.

"Please don't be upset," the pilot went on. "We have lowered the plane's wheels manually, but there is a chance that the wheels will collapse when we land at Los Angeles. We have radioed ahead for emergency vehicles to be standing by, and we will be announcing precautions to take for your own safety."

She switched off, and the babbling turned into an uproar. As the flight attendants tried desperately to settle people down, I stared out at the orange light of a spectacular sunset. *The sun is dying*, I thought, and something clenched in my stomach.

Aunt Melody patted the back of my hand and I managed a feeble smile. "I guess I was right."

"What about, Liz?"

"When I said the attendant was tense. She already knew about the hydraulic gear."

"You're probably right. I suppose they had to act normally and serve us our dinners until the pilot made her announcement close to the end."

"The end." I couldn't smile anymore. "Oh, Aunt Melody, I'm scared."

"So am I, dear."

Kingsley sat down beside her. The shock of the pilot's

announcement had drained most of the colour from his face, and he looked ghastly. "How are you doing?"

"Just fine, Kingsley. And you?"

"Couldn't be better! This airline is the best in the States. They'll get us down safely."

The attendant came out of nowhere to collect our dinner trays, and I saw that her hands weren't shaking anymore. Maybe she'd only been afraid of leaking the awful news to the passengers. She even gave me a smile, and somehow that really raised my spirits.

"Pardon me," Aunt Melody said to her. "Why didn't we land earlier, instead of flying on to Los Angeles?"

"There are more ambulances available there."

"Oh."

What can you say to a line like that? I didn't want to believe this was happening to me, so I managed to make myself think about all the Disneyland attractions for quite a long time, maybe as long as eight seconds.

"I was right about a disaster," I said to Kingsley. "The engine didn't fall off, but this is just as bad."

He gave a feeble smile. "Nonsense, Liz. In a few minutes we'll land at Los Angeles, and it will all be over."

"All over is right. You know what'll happen the moment we land? As the wheels touch the runway, they'll collapse. The plane will skid along on its belly, with sparks flying in every direction. Then the fuel tanks will rip open, the fuel will ignite, and there'll be a massive explosion. One minute a plane, the next minute a fireball! There won't be anything left of us, Kingsley! We've had it, we're finished! Say goodbye to life!"

Suddenly I noticed that heads were turning in my direction and people close by were crying. Realizing I'd gotten a bit carried away, I tried to smile. "Don't listen to me, folks. I'm only a kid."

"Not just any kid," Aunt Melody said. "When it comes to flying, you're a totally paranoid kid. And I guess this experience isn't going to improve things."

The pilot's voice came over the speakers. "We're approaching Los Angeles Airport. The attendants are now handing out small brown bags. Please put your jewellery and all sharp objects into a bag and label it with your name."

Where did the bags come from, I wondered. Did every plane carry them in case of a crash? These morbid thoughts ran through my mind as I looked at a thin line of red stretching across the horizon. High above was a pale quarter-moon just coming to life, and below was nothing but darkness.

The attendant handed each of us a pillow. "Put this in your lap. A minute before we land, the pilot will ask everyone to assume the emergency position."

"Which is?"

"Hands clasped behind your head and your face in the pillow. Stay that way until the plane has come to a full stop."

We're going to make it safely, I told myself, and I don't want to feel ashamed when it's over. Did I ever intend to enjoy Disneyland!

"Good luck," the attendant said. "There's no need to worry."

"Well," Aunt Melody said, "at least we're all in this together. Literally."

The attendant laughed. "You're right! I'll pass that on to the Captain."

Outside the window, the sky changed suddenly to night as we dropped toward Los Angeles. The city streets were shining with neon, and they seemed to go on forever. I glimpsed a massive freeway, at least twenty lanes, then the plane swept into a curve and I looked across dusky houses and bright streets to the blood-red sea.

Were people down there watching us? We were probably

on TV, all the cameras angling up to catch the drama as our wheels came down closer and closer to the runway. What would happen then?

A neon sign was flashing in time with my heart, then it went blurry as my eyes started leaking. We were really low now, and there was a sudden roar from the engines as the plane dipped forward.

"Assume your emergency positions!" the pilot announced.

I buried my head in the pillow, then looked up. "I love you, Aunt Melody," I sobbed.

She smiled. "I love you, too, Liz. We're going to be fine."

I tried to say something more, but then the plane dropped straight down. I grabbed the back of my head and jammed my face into the pillow.

There was a loud thump as the wheels hit the runway, followed immediately by the tremendous roar of the afterburners slowing the engines. I held my breath and prayed and prayed, waiting for the terrible screech of collapsing metal, but nothing like that happened. Instead there was a moment of silence inside the plane, followed by hysterical cheering and laughter and applause.

I looked up and saw two people in the aisle hugging each other. Then I got into the act, wrapping my arms around Aunt Melody and squeezing her so tightly that I thought she'd pop. After that I remembered Kingsley, and realized this was a golden opportunity to put my arms around *him*. But when I looked his way I got a real shock.

Kingsley had fainted.

2

I couldn't believe it.

Kingsley Fortune, probably the most perfect man in the U.S.A., had fainted dead away. After a moment his eyes flickered open. "Are we okay?" he whispered.

"Absolutely fine," Aunt Melody replied briskly. "As you said, this is your nation's finest airline. The pilot deserves a medal."

Kingsley leaned back in his seat, breathing heavily. Then he looked at me with those deep blue eyes. "I guess I'm no hero, Liz. Sorry."

"I couldn't care less, Kingsley! Everybody was scared stiff and I was crying like a baby. But I'll tell you something. I'm *walking* home to Winnipeg."

He smiled. "Perhaps I'll see you two before you leave. What are your plans?"

Aunt Melody stood up. "We haven't decided."

"Where are you staying?"

"A motel somewhere in Anaheim. I don't remember the name."

What? I knew that Aunt Melody had the motel's name in her pocket, yet she was deliberately ignoring the chance to see Kingsley again. I stared at her, then quickly got out *my* itinerary and told Kingsley the name of the motel. "We're going on the movie studio tour tomorrow," I added helpfully. "You know, Universal City."

"Wonderful place. I insist on being your escort."

"Great! We accept."

Aunt Melody flashed me a dagger look, but I pretended not to notice. Maybe she was turned off Kingsley for the moment, but by tomorrow she'd want to see him again. Luckily for her, I'd snatched victory from the jaws of defeat, so to speak.

Inside the airport there was total bedlam. Relatives of people coming off the plane were crying, reporters were grabbing people for interviews, and everyone in the crowd was shoving each other around, trying to get a good view of the "survivors." I felt like a real celebrity, and was dying to be interviewed, but Aunt Melody hustled me through the crowd and out of the terminal.

I'd hoped for a ride to the motel from Kingsley, but he volunteered for a TV interview, and the last I'd seen of him, his golden hair was lit by strobe lights as he described the tension of the last moments before the plane touched down.

So we were stuck with travelling by bus, but it was exciting just the same. Los Angeles is such a massive city that it took at least an hour to reach Anaheim, where Disneyland is located, and our bus must have used about eight different freeways to get there. I didn't mind, though, because I was too busy staring at all the traffic and the fantastic neon light show from all the signs we passed.

Then came the thrilling moment when I spotted a red sign with the famous words *Disneyland Hotel.* I guess it was like seeing the Taj Mahal or something, and I sat straight up and grabbed Aunt Melody's arm.

"Look! We've actually made it to Disneyland!"

The bus pulled up in front of the hotel's driveway, and seconds later a monorail glided in and stopped above our heads. It was like something out of a space movie, with its long silver body and flashing coloured lights, and I wanted desperately to go for a ride.

"Couldn't we stay at the Disneyland Hotel, Aunt Melody? Just for one night? I'll pay for my share, I promise."

She smiled. "We couldn't afford to rent a broom closet here, Liz. Maybe we'll come over one day and walk around."

"We've got to see it! My friends told me this place even has its own lagoon, if you can believe it."

The bus driver explained that the monorail took hotel guests to Disneyland, which was close by. But it was too dark for us to see it, so we grabbed a taxi to our motel a few blocks away, and pretty soon I was trying all the different Los Angeles TV channels. After that I stood in the warm night air on our balcony, listening to the big leaves of the palm trees rattling together in the wind.

I thought the morning would *never* come.

But it did, thank goodness. I was up long before Aunt Melody, hanging over the balcony watching all those California people pass on Katella Avenue. A good-looking guy went by driving an old hearse with a surfboard in the back, then there was a Hell's Angel on a candy-apple red bike, and I saw this gorgeous woman driving a sports car with her long blond hair streaming in the wind. I'll bet any money she was a star, on her way to the studio.

We ate at the Hamburger House (though Aunt Melody refused to let me have a cheeseburger for breakfast) and then

Kingsley arrived driving a battered old Chev, which was kind of disappointing. Not that I'm a snob, but somehow I'd had visions of a long black limousine with a cute chauffeur wearing shades, and a stereo system with individual controls. I had my camera all set to get a picture of the limo, so instead I asked Aunt Melody to take one of me with Kingsley. When he put his arm around me, I felt much better!

We piled into the car and headed for the Santa Ana Freeway. I asked Kingsley why there are so many Spanish names in California, and he told us how the King of Spain had once owned all this land, and how the city was founded as *el pueblo de nuestra señora la reina de los angeles*, which means City of Our Lady, Queen of the Angels. No wonder it's called L.A. for short!

There were some pretty mountains to the north, but I had to laugh when the freeway crossed a concrete channel and Kingsley insisted on calling it a river. He said heavy rains could turn the "rivers" into raging torrents, so they paved them to prevent flooding, but I just couldn't feature that dribble of brown water as a flood.

During the whole drive Aunt Melody was strangely quiet, but I couldn't figure out what was bothering her. Kingsley did his best, pointing out all the sights like the famous HOLLY-WOOD sign, and a hotel made of golden glass which actually has a stream running through the lobby, but he couldn't make a dent.

"On Sunday I'm going to my drive-in church," he said. "You two interested?"

"A drive-in church? What do you mean?"

"The church has a glass wall overlooking the parking lot. You can see the preacher talking to the congregation inside the church, and his voice comes to you on speakers."

Aunt Melody glanced at Kingsley. "Do you attend church regularly?"

"Yes."

Aunt Melody didn't say anything more, but I could tell she had softened toward Kingsley. She's a deeply religious person. Trying to keep her good mood alive, I tossed in a joke.

"Kingsley, do you eat chicken with your fingers?"

"Sure."

"How sick. Most people just eat the chicken."

Kingsley really laughed, and so did Aunt Melody, even though she'd heard the joke a few times before. Excellent progress! I was searching my memory bank for some more yuks when we left the freeway and headed up the side of a green hill.

"We're approaching Universal Studios," Kingsley said. "This is a real movie studio, so there may be some famous stars strolling around. You can't go into the sound stages during filming, but there's a tour on a tram through the Back Lot where they demonstrate special effects like the parting of the Red Sea."

"Are we going to see Jaws?"

"You bet, but don't lean too close to the water or they'll be calling you the headless kid."

Aunt Melody looked at Kingsley. "A friend of mine said visitors are chosen to act scenes from the movie *Airport*, with a whole audience watching."

"That's right," he said. "Besides the Back Lot tour, you get free admission to several special shows. One is the filming of *Airport*, and another is the Cowboy Stunt Show, where cowboys fall off buildings and that kind of thing."

"What's your favourite show, Kingsley?"

"Castle Dracula."

"Wow. What's that?"

"Tell you in a second," Kingsley replied, as he manoeuvred into a parking space. The lot was one of the biggest I'd ever seen, and it was jammed with tour buses. As we walked to the ticket office I saw a bus from Alberta with a sign reading

CANADA so much to go for. That made me feel good, I guess because I was feeling a little bit homesick, but I quickly got used to seeing people wearing maple-leaf pins and badges and hats. Half the population of Canada must have been at Universal City that day.

As soon as we were inside the gate, I started pestering Kingsley about Castle Dracula. "Is it real? Do we get to explore it, or what?"

He laughed. "We'd better go to the Castle first. There's a show starting in ten minutes."

As we hurried past the entrances to the other shows, Kingsley explained that we'd be sitting in a banquet hall where Dracula entertained his guests. "Some of them are pretty strange creatures, Liz. Feeling brave?"

"You bet! I can hardly wait."

We entered Castle Dracula through a stone archway, and found some seats. Then I just stared and stared. It was totally creepy. Mournful organ music was playing, and the windows were lit by flashes of lightning. In front of me was a long table set for a feast, with silver candlesticks and a white tablecloth embroidered with Count Dracula's coat-of-arms. But there was no sign of any guests.

In fact there was no sign of life at all, just the sound of howling werewolves and giant spider webs moving against the stone walls. Torches flickered and snarling gargoyles crouched around the banquet hall. But where was Dracula? I'd just started whispering to Aunt Melody when I heard him.

"Silence, mortals!" he said in a voice that gave me the shivers. "How dare you enter the sanctuary of the Prince of Darkness."

There was still no sign of Dracula, just his voice, and then a trap door creaked open in the floor and this weirdo crawled out wearing a striped prison outfit.

"This is my minion, Renfield," Dracula's voice said. "He feeds on insects, like that nice fat snack he has in his hand."

Renfield held a wriggling, hairy tarantula in his hand. Suddenly the maniac cackled, and ran straight at me with the giant spider! I screamed and buried my face in Aunt Melody's side.

Everyone laughed, and Aunt Melody hugged me, but I still didn't look up for a minute. When I did, Renfield was squatting on a chair at the table and the tarantula was gone. Had he eaten it?

I looked at Aunt Melody. "Should we get out of here? I'm terrified of spiders, and that guy makes my skin crawl."

She smiled. "I thought you were full of courageous Austen family blood."

"You're right. And I intend to keep it inside *me*."

Kingsley laughed. "I'll protect you, Liz."

Suddenly, at the top of some wide stone stairs, Dracula appeared. He was younger than I expected and really handsome, with long black hair and beautiful dark eyes, but I still shuddered as he swept his cape over his shoulder and came slowly down the stairs.

"Where has this rabble come from? How dare you permit them to intrude upon my feast?" Reaching the table, he lifted that little Renfield jerk into the air and held him there, gibbering and spluttering.

Dropping Renfield, Dracula started walking toward me. I grabbed Aunt Melody and held on tight, but fortunately he went past and stopped at a blond girl.

"I am Count Dracula," he said in that creepy voice. "Would you care to join me for dinner?"

Like a fool, the girl stood up. Holding her hand, Dracula led her to the top of the stone staircase and then stopped. The organ music started going BAROOM! BAROOM! BAROOM! and the werewolves went crazy outside the castle windows, howling and gnashing their teeth.

I couldn't help trembling with excitement as Dracula bent to kiss her neck. After that he covered her with his cape and they both disappeared into thin air.

Renfield giggled hysterically, then turned and stared at me with his beady little eyes. "If *he* tries to kiss me," I whispered to Aunt Melody, "he'll get a swift one in the chops."

"You tell him, Liz," she said, patting my hand.

There was a tremendous crash as someone drove his fist through a wooden door in the castle wall. Renfield scuttled over to open the door, and in came Frankenstein and a girl with a chalk-white face who must have been his bride. They clumped to the table, dropped down into chairs, and began grabbing at the food and wine. Renfield tried to make them behave but failed hopelessly. Then Dracula was back, bringing his bride to the feast. She looked *horrible*. Her blond hair had turned pitch-black, her face was white, and a trickle of blood ran down from her black lips.

After Dracula had led her to the table, all kinds of action broke out with various monsters breaking into the castle and Dracula trying to get rid of them. To tell the truth, I didn't follow the story very carefully because I was staring at Dracula's bride, wondering what it would feel like to be one of the undead. I can't help it, I believe in vampires.

Then it was all over. Dracula made a final appearance on a balcony, warning us he would live forever and would be back, looking for fresh blood, and then he was gone. I felt kind of empty, and was just sitting there staring into space when a woman appeared with a clipboard.

"Would anyone like to take part in the next performance?" she asked. "We need some actors."

I jumped straight up. "Me! Me! Me!" I shouted, waving my arms. "Pick me!"

I guess I embarrassed Aunt Melody, because I heard some kind of strangled sounds from her direction, but I just kept waving my arms and jumping around. Fortunately the woman spotted me and wrote down my name.

"Come back at 1:30," she said, "and we'll do your make-up before the next show."

"Can I be Dracula's bride? *Please!*"

"Yup."

I could hardly believe I was going to star at Castle Dracula. Maybe there'd be a talent scout in the audience, and they'd sign me for a major movie. Would Tom ever be jealous!

I was so excited I could hardly concentrate on the next part of our visit, which was the tram ride through the Back Lot to see the special effects. Kingsley skipped the ride because he'd seen it all before, but we had so much fun I hardly missed him. Notice I said hardly!

The best part of the tour was the tumbling ride through the heart of a glacier, when it seemed like I was going to fall out of the tram, but Aunt Melody's favourite was Jaws, who swallowed a fisherman and then took a flying leap at us.

When we were safely away from Jaws, I smiled at Aunt Melody. "Too bad Kingsley wasn't here to protect us."

Aunt Melody shook her head. "I wouldn't get your hopes up about Kingsley, Liz. For some reason I don't trust that man. I..."

"You think he's some kind of a crook?"

"Of course not. Why do you ask that?"

"There must be some reason why you don't like such a beautiful hunk. Is it because he says he's always been an actor, when he's got all those callouses?"

"That's part of it." Aunt Melody hesitated. "He phoned last night, after you were asleep. At first I thought he wanted to take me out, but he never mentioned that."

"What did he talk about?"

"My singing in Minneapolis, and why I'd come to Los Angeles. He didn't seem to believe we're just on a holiday. He seemed to be fishing around for something."

"Maybe he wants you as co-star in his next flick."

Aunt Melody laughed. "That'll be the day. My advice to you, Liz, is to take everything Kingsley says with a large grain of salt."

I have great faith in Aunt Melody and how she feels about people, so I confess I was bothered by her doubts about Kingsley. They were still nagging me when the tour ended with some inside information about special effects (like how actors use cigarette smoke to make their breath look cold when they're filming a winter scene in the middle of the summer), but I forgot them as I raced off to Castle Dracula for my make-up.

I was really excited, but as soon as I got inside the make-up room my heart started pounding. What if I blew it? Here I was surrounded by professionals — the director, the make-up people, the other actors — and they were all counting on me to do my part properly. I started sweating, and was even thinking of sneaking out the door when a make-up girl nodded at me.

"Sit here, please," she said, pointing at a big padded chair in front of a mirror completely surrounded by light bulbs.

It was too late to back out, so I climbed into the chair and tried to calm my nerves by looking around. It was actually very exciting, because everything looked just like you'd expect in Hollywood, with jars of make-up everywhere and funny little cartoons stuck in the sides of the mirror and people bustling all over the place. One of the monsters was the nicest, stopping to ask if I was enjoying Universal City, but I was most surprised by Renfield, who turned out to be an average-sized guy and really friendly. Not the shrivelled little runt I'd seen on stage. That's the magic of Hollywood!

In the chair next to me was another girl about my age who was going to be Frankenstein's bride. She looked just as nervous as I was, which made me feel better, so I smiled at her.

"Do you wish you hadn't volunteered?"

"Yes!" she exclaimed. "I'm terrified."

The boy who was doing her make-up smiled. "You'll enjoy the show. It's lots of fun."

"I just wish it was over," the girl said, and I nodded in agreement.

Getting made up was a complicated process. It started with having thick white powder brushed all over my face. Then the girl carefully applied black eyeshadow and black lipstick, followed by a serpent's tongue of red blood running from the corner of my mouth down past my chin. I put on long white gloves that had sharp fingernails which clicked together, then pulled a gown over my t-shirt and jeans, added a wig of scraggly black hair and looked in the mirror.

The thing that looked back was *gruesome*.

I had become the blood-chilling image of a ghoul, ready to prowl the countryside in search of graveyards. My heart thumped as I stared at the white face and black hair in the mirror. Now I was one of the undead.

Somewhere the organ started playing, and the room shook with the sound of thunder. "Five minutes everyone!" the director shouted, then looked at me. "Got your ear-plug?"

"My what?"

She turned angrily to the make-up girl, who hurried over with a little black button. "Sorry, Francine. I forgot."

"That's okay." She pushed aside my thick black hair and shoved the button into my ear. "That's for your instructions," she said, and hurried out of the room.

"What instructions?" I yelped. "Hey, wait a minute!"

"Places everyone!" some guy shouted.

We were all hustled into a dark passage behind the stage, and I stood there listening to the pounding of the organ and the pounding of my heart. *What instructions?*

Then my ear exploded with noise. "Bride of Dracula! Get ready!"

I practically jumped out of my costume. When I had calmed down, I realized the director was going to radio her instructions to me through the ear-plug. So that's how it worked! No problem! Feeling cool and confident *at last,* I turned to Frankenstein's bride.

"Break a leg," I grinned.

Her black lips smiled. "Good luck."

"No! Don't say that!"

"Why?"

"You've just jinxed my performance!"

"What?"

Before I could explain, Dracula appeared in the passage with a girl from the audience. She giggled some stupid remark about the way he'd kissed her neck, then she was hustled away by the assistant director and I took her place at Dracula's side.

"You look charming," he said, smiling at me with those gorgeous dark eyes. "I'm sure you'll be the best bride of all."

"Impossible," I groaned. "Someone just wished me good luck."

"Oh, no!"

Even though he squeezed my hand sympathetically, I think we both knew I was doomed. A velvet curtain parted and I walked out with Dracula onto the stone staircase.

"Bride of Dracula! Turn and sm#*****%#kkl%####jfe."

The jinx! It was actually happening! The director's words had turned to static inside my ear and I couldn't understand what I was supposed to do. My body went ice cold and I stared dumbly up at Dracula. Fortunately he seemed to understand I was in trouble, and murmured soothing words as he led me down the staircase.

"Just stay in character," he said. "Be my bride at all times."

"But what . . . ?"

"Sssh!" he warned. "The audience may hear."

Trying to look dignified, I approached the table and stopped. Should I pull out the chair, or wait for Dracula to do it? Somewhere in a hidden booth the director must have seen me hesitate.

"Bride o##%%$kekel! op#% d%#fgh!"

As my eyes scanned the audience, I saw Aunt Melody sitting beside Kingsley, and I just about died. Of all the people in the world, he was the last one I wanted to witness my public humiliation. Somehow I kept from running off the stage as a great bubble of panic rose inside me. Terrified, I turned to stare at Renfield, crouching on his chair. *Help me, Renfield!*

From behind, Dracula spoke. "Sit down, my beauty. How wise of you to insist that I display some manners." He held out the chair and I sank down. My whole body was quivering and I felt as if I was going to faint.

"##oodl#% p%%#&l wine!"

Wine? At last, a word I could understand. Desperately I reached for a silver goblet, but my hand was shaking so badly that the coloured liquid splattered all over the white tablecloth. Someone in the audience laughed, and tears rose in my eyes.

Be brave, I told myself.

Easier said than done. The action was whirling all around me and I was dimly aware of monsters racing past and spiders crawling along the table and screams from the audience, but all my attention was on the hated ear-plug and the unknown words spluttering from it. Once I thought I heard the word "food" and reached timidly for my knife and fork, then paused. Surely Dracula's bride would crave nothing but blood? Slowly I returned my hands to my lap, while the ear-plug vibrated with wild shouts.

Then, *finally*, from somewhere behind me I heard Dracula's parting words to the audience.

Thank goodness it was over! But how was I supposed to get off the stage? Would Dracula return to escort me? Frankenstein and his bride clumped away while I sat at the table looking like an idiot.

"Br####%ss lll%if %%%**lloofphrig!"

The house lights went up and some of the audience started shuffling away, but others sensed something was wrong. I could see faces staring, while some people whispered and pointed at me. Refusing to look in Kingsley's direction, I lowered my head and fought back tears.

Then Dracula was beside me, holding out his hand. "Come along, my beauty. We must return to our graves, for the dawn is breaking."

Never had I been happier to see another person. Stumbling out of the chair I grabbed Dracula's arm and held tight as we climbed the stairs. The moment we reached the dark passage behind the stage I started crying.

"Hey, take it easy," Dracula said. "You did fine."

"No, I didn't! I was a useless *mess*!"

Frankenstein's bride came along the passage and put her arm around my shoulders. "What's wrong?"

"I wrecked everything," I blubbered. "I let all the actors down and the director and everyone! But it wasn't my fault. I couldn't understand anything the director said."

Dracula nodded. "I thought your ear-plug wasn't working properly. It went haywire once before, something about battery corrosion."

"You mean this happened to someone else?"

"Sure. And anyway, you were just fine out there. The show wasn't spoiled in the slightest."

"You mean nobody's mad at me?"

He laughed. "Of course not."

"Thank goodness!" I said, then reached out and gave him the biggest hug. After all, he was really cute, so why miss a chance? Then I turned to Frankenstein's bride and hugged her, too. I guess I needed some comforting.

"What's your name?" she asked, as we walked to the make-up room with our arms around each other like life-long buddies.

"Liz Austen, and I'm from Canada. How about you?"

"My name is Serena Hernandez. I live in San Francisco right now, but my country is La Luceña. Do you know it?"

"We studied something about La Luceña in current events. Aren't people fighting there?"

"Some are," she said, smiling. "It's a beautiful country. You must come and visit me some time."

"I'd love to, Serena. And you've got to visit me in Winnipeg."

Well, within a few minutes we were close friends. I got rid of my gown and wig and that horrible ear-plug, but they let us keep our make-up on. As soon as we left Castle Dracula people started doing double-takes. Their eyes popped out of their heads and I saw some little kids grab their parents and start crying. I guess our white faces and black eyes and the blood dribbling from our lips was a bit too much for them. It was fantastic!

Aunt Melody and Kingsley appeared, and right away Aunt Melody hugged me. I guess she knew what I'd been through. Then Kingsley shook my hand and offered congratulations.

"You were splendid, the way you came down the staircase on the count's arm. So regal. I got goosebumps watching you."

"Really?" I said, wanting desperately to believe him. "But what about when I spilled the wine?"

"Wasn't that part of the act? I thought you'd reached for some blood, then tossed it aside when you realized it was only wine. I thought it was a nice character touch."

"Oh!" I said, grinning happily. "Well, all right!"

So everything was just fine. I introduced Serena, who explained that she and her father were on holiday staying at the Disneyland Hotel. I was just about dying of envy, and finally got up the nerve to ask if I could visit her at the hotel.

"Come over tonight," Serena said. "I'll tell my father I want you to be my guest for dinner."

"I couldn't do that, Serena. It's too expensive."

"Nonsense. He can afford it, and I insist."

I hoped Kingsley would grab the chance to invite Aunt

Melody out for dinner, but for some reason he didn't. Instead he suggested going to Disneyland with us, and we agreed.

If it hadn't been for a little toad, the day at Universal City would have been perfect. Not a toad, actually, but a boy who looked just like one. His eyes bulged out of his warty head and his clothes were filled with fat.

He walked right up to me and said, "You were Dracula's bride. You were lousy."

My feelings were really hurt, and for a second I just stared at his ugly little eyes. Then I took a swing at him but he hopped backwards and stuck out his tongue.

"Ignore him," Serena said, then turned to the Toad. "Get out of here, Ramón. Go find your mother."

"She got eaten by Jaws, so now I belong to you."

Serena said something in Spanish that sounded pretty rude, but the Toad just laughed. At that moment a woman with black hair and beautiful olive-coloured skin came up behind the Toad and put her hands on his shoulders.

"Are you behaving yourself, Ramón?"

"Of course, Mama."

The woman glanced at Serena. "You look wonderful in that make-up, Serena."

"I'm actually supposed to look ghastly, but thanks anyway, Señora Garcia. This is my friend from Canada, Liz Austen."

"Pleased to meet you, Liz."

"Señora Garcia is Vice-consul for La Luceña. She works with my father."

"Is he here?"

Serena shook her head. "He didn't come with us today because he's visiting a friend in the hospital."

Señora Garcia looked at her. "Please take care of Ramón for an hour. He's so exhausting, I need a rest."

Turning, she walked quickly away. At the same time, the

Toad grabbed Serena's hand and started dragging her toward the Airport show.

"It's starting!" he shouted. "Come on, I don't wanna miss it. Hurry up, Serena, move your stupid feet!"

For a moment I was glad to see that human disaster zone disappear into the crowd with Serena, but then I felt sorry for her. Quickly arranging to meet Aunt Melody later, I caught up with Serena as she looked for seats.

"I'll keep you company, Serena."

The Toad aimed a kick at me, but missed. "I don't want you around. Beat it."

"You want something beat?" I said, giving his ear a twist. "I'll beat your head into the ground, you little creep."

"Ow! Let go!"

"Beg for forgiveness."

"No!"

I twisted harder. "Beg!"

"Ow! Help! Ow! Forgive me!"

"Don't cross me again," I said, releasing him, "or I'll feed you to my boa constrictor."

The Toad's eyes glittered angrily as he rubbed his ear. Then he took a run at me but Serena grabbed the brat and wrestled him into a seat, shouting something in Spanish. The Toad calmed right down, and I looked at Serena in surprise as I sat beside her.

"What did you say?"

"I threatened to tell you his secret."

"Wow! What is it?"

The Toad wiggled anxiously, and Serena laughed. "I'd better not tell you, Liz. It's my only weapon against him."

"Please, Serena. I've got to know! Isn't he toilet trained or something?"

Serena grinned and the Toad shook his fist in my direction.

Before I could say anything more there was a dramatic drum roll and a man ran onto the stage carrying a mike. "Welcome to the filming of an actual movie, ladies and gentlemen! First of all, we need some volunteers to be our stars."

People leapt up all over the place, behaving like idiots as they tried to attract his attention. A middle-aged man stood on his seat wiggling his hips and pointing to himself, and some other guy was waving money in the air. I couldn't believe it! Meanwhile Serena and I were acting like proper ladies, except maybe for our screams.

But we were ignored, and the lucky people headed for the stage. They were sent to various locations, like the inside of a cut-away jet, and given instructions by the director. Then cameras rolled into place and the filming started.

It was great! The volunteers were a bunch of hams and didn't seem to care about making fools of themselves as they were ordered to yell and faint when their jet made a crash-landing and sank to the sea bed. Eventually the navy raised the plane to the surface and the survivors were herded onto the wing.

On a separate set, cameras zoomed in on a man and woman as they appeared in a doorway overlooking a huge tank of sea water. "Okay!" the director shouted to them. "Jump!"

"Jump?" one of them called in a strangled voice. "Into that water?"

"That's right! Hurry up, the cameras are rolling."

"We'll get soaked!"

"Doesn't matter! Hollywood expects her stars to be brave."

The woman leaned forward, hesitating, then shook her head and turned away. But the man grabbed her and jumped. The pair landed with an incredible splash and, through the tank's glass sides, we saw them thrash to the surface in their soaked clothes. Climbing out of the tank they managed to grin, and the audience gave them a big hand.

The director signalled for quiet. "Now the *really* big thrill, ladies and gentlemen! In a few minutes you will see the actual movie that has just been filmed."

"Wow, Serena, isn't this great? I wonder what it'll be like?"

But I never found out. The Toad suddenly took off, Serena went after him, and I reluctantly joined the chase. The kid moved faster than a greased pig, and we didn't catch up until he'd reached the Cowboy Stunt Show.

"Airport was a drag," he announced, as we dropped down into some seats, gasping. "You shouldn't have taken me there."

"It was your idea," Serena protested.

"No, it wasn't. You're always lying, Serena."

I leaned toward the Toad. "What's your favourite brand?"

"Huh?"

"Is it Pampers?"

He looked at Serena. "Who is this fool?"

"Come on, Ramón," I said, smiling. "Don't be afraid to tell me. Which diapers do you recommend to all your friends?"

"I'll get you, you pimple," he said, with fury in his little black eyes. "Say your prayers."

Grinning, I settled back to study the buildings from the Old West where the cowboys would be doing their show. Then I turned to look at the people around us, and got a shock.

Once again I was being stared at by the same woman.

She was incredibly beautiful, with big dark eyes and high cheekbones, and hair so black you'd think it was dyed except for the way it glistened in the sun. Somehow you'd expect someone that gorgeous to be dressed in imported silk, but in fact she was wearing a wrinkled cotton blouse and faded old jeans without any jewellery.

I'd first noticed her on the fringes of the crowd after the Castle Dracula show, when we'd been spooking people with our make-up. At first, I thought she'd been staring at the make-up, but later I'd seen her at the *Airport* Show, and she was still at it.

And now here she was again, with her enormous eyes on me. I tried staring back, then leaned close to Serena and told her what was happening.

"Do you know her?"

She shook her head. "Maybe she's going to sign you to a Hollywood contract."

"Not just me, Serena. She's been staring at you, too, and the Toad."

"Well, I won't sign for less than a million."

"Maybe she wants the Toad for that new horror movie they're doing. *It Came From Under the Sink.*"

"I heard the movie's called *My Eyes Bulge Coz My Pampers Are Too Tight.*"

"Funny," the Toad muttered. "You two are a real laugh riot."

I looked over at the woman. Now she was leaning back, pretending not to notice us. "That person is worth investigating. If my brother Tom was here, we'd give her the third degree."

The Toad snorted. "I suppose you think you're a detective."

"As a matter of fact, I am."

The Toad's nostrils bulged as he snorted again. "If you're a detective, I'm the Lone Ranger."

"Boy, you sure are the Jerk of the Century." I turned to Serena. "Are you sure you can't tell me anything about that woman? I've got a feeling she's deliberately following us."

Serena shook her head. "It's just a coincidence, Liz."

"Then I wonder if she's a spy, or maybe a courier for a diamond-smuggling operation."

The Toad stood up. "There's only one way to find out if she's a spy or a diamond smuggler. I'll go ask her."

"Don't you *dare*!" I shouted, making a grab at him. But he

wriggled away, and seconds later was standing in front of the woman, saying something and pointing my way. She looked surprised, and her lips formed the word *spy?* The Toad nodded his stupid little head, grinning, and they both started laughing.

"That reptile," I said angrily. "That little pop-eyed crawling lizard. He'll regret the day he crossed Liz Austen."

"Wow, you really are mad. What are you going to do?"

"Is the Toad staying at the Disneyland Hotel, too?"

Serena nodded.

"Then I'll get him tonight. I just happen to have the perfect revenge tucked away in my suitcase for a rainy day. That little sucker will never know what hit him."

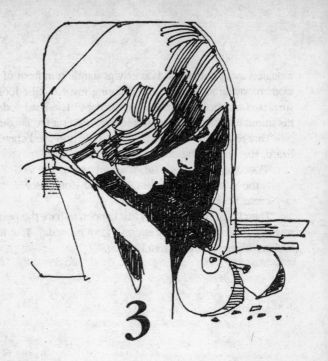

3

A few hours later I was at the Disneyland Hotel.

If you've ever been there, you'll know it's more like a city than a hotel. There are several high-rise towers with bedrooms, then there are all the stores and video arcades in special shopping malls, huge swimming pools and even a *sea* with war canoes and trimarans sailing around in front of temples and adobe huts.

Serena was waiting for me in the lobby of the Bonita Tower, wearing an outfit that must have cost a medium-sized fortune. My face went beet-red because I was just wearing a sweater and jeans, and I absolutely refused Serena's idea that we eat in a fancy dining room.

We ended up in the coffee shop, which was full of ordinary people in ordinary clothes, and I began to relax. Especially when I studied a glass case displaying about ten cakes, including a big fat chocolate one topped with vanilla icing and huge maraschino cherries.

"That's what I want! Would your dad mind?"

Serena laughed. "Not at all. He expected to be paying for pheasant and caviar and Baked Alaska."

"Really?" For a moment I regretted missing the chance, but no way would I wear my old jeans into an expensive restaurant and have everyone stare. "What's your dad's job, Serena? I don't know what a consul is."

"He represents our country in California. He tries to convince American companies to start businesses in La Luceña, and helps people from home who run into problems here."

"Why are people fighting each other in La Luceña?"

Serena shrugged. "Some want to get rid of the government."

"Why don't they wait for the election?"

"I guess there hasn't been an election for a long time, but I don't know much about it. Papa hasn't mentioned the fighting since we moved to the States."

"Who do you think that woman was today? The one who was following us?"

Serena smiled. "You were imagining things, Liz. She just happened to be at the same shows as us."

"Is your dad wealthy?"

"Sort of, I guess. Why?"

"Maybe you're going to be taken hostage, and held for a huge ransom. A girl I know in Winnipeg got kidnapped, but my brother found her in the basement of some old house. Dianne said it was really horrible. She thought the kidnappers were going to kill her."

"So you were serious about you two being detectives. What a family!"

I laughed. "Tom's not bad. Sometimes I let him assist me on a case."

"Why isn't he here with you?"

"Aunt Melody could only afford to treat one of us to a vacation, so Mom and Dad decided it was my turn for a holiday. They once sent Tom on the train to Vancouver, but he got mixed up in a murder case and was nearly blown away. Even though my Dad's a police officer, my parents weren't too pleased."

"I'll bet. Tom sounds a lot more interesting than the Toad."

"Speaking of that walking wart, I've brought him a little present." I pointed to a package I'd put on the counter where we were sitting. "You think he's a bundle of energy now? After we've finished with him, he won't sit still for a week."

Serena's eyes lit up. "What's in the package?"

"Tell you soon." As the waitress arrived with an egg-salad sandwich my mouth watered hungrily and I quickly took several bites and followed up with some skim milk.

"Why do you drink that stuff?" Serena asked. "It looks horrid."

"I used to get zits from drinking regular milk, I guess because of all the cream. When I switched to skim they disappeared."

"Maybe I should switch," Serena said, reaching for her chocolate milkshake.

"Why bother?" I said mournfully, looking at her smooth dark skin and glowing black hair. "You're already perfect. By the way, who's in that locket you're wearing?"

"My mother, and my sister."

"How come they didn't come to Disneyland with you?"

"They're dead."

For a moment I was too stunned to say anything, then I mumbled something about how Serena must miss them. She nodded and went on drinking her milkshake, while I tried to think of something else to talk about.

"Where ... uh ... what's your school like?"

"I don't mind talking about my mother and my sister,"

Serena said. "One morning they got into the car outside our home in La Luceña. Mother turned on the engine, and the car blew up. Papa and I were still inside, collecting our lunches or something, so we escaped being killed."

"Why did the car blow up?"

"A bomb was connected to the starter."

"But *why*? Who'd do something like that?"

"The people who are trying to bring down the government. They'll do anything to get their way."

There was a lot more I wanted to ask Serena, but I didn't feel I had the right. But now I understood why she seemed so mature for her age. For a moment I pictured myself in Winnipeg, getting ready for school with Mom outside warming up the car, then I shuddered. It seemed impossible that something like that could happen, yet it had happened to Serena.

My order of chocolate cake appeared before me, but I'd lost my appetite. I was staring at the other people in the coffee shop, wondering how they could possibly be laughing and having fun, when Serena smiled.

"Cheer up, Liz! I miss Mama and my sister dreadfully, but I'm still enjoying my life. I've only got one, you know, so I want to use it well. Tell me what's in that package for the Toad."

With a real effort I made myself smile. "Itching powder."

"Fabulous! Have you got a plan?"

"Nope. We just grab him and pour the itching powder inside his clothes. The powder has tiny hairs that will get stuck in the pores of his skin and itch like crazy. He'll jump around like his shoes are on fire!"

"Let's go find him!"

"Just a sec," I said, holding up my hand. "Can your dad afford an apple?"

"Of course."

"Then may I tell your fortune?"

The waitress brought us an apple and I handed it to Serena along with a sharp knife. "Cut the apple in half. The number of pips you find in the core is the number of years until you get married."

As Serena sliced apart the apple and started counting, I stared in shock at the core. Somehow she'd cut three pips in half, which was an extremely bad omen. I could have kicked myself for suggesting the apple. I tried to pretend it was only a silly superstition, but in my heart I knew that something really terrible lay waiting soon in Serena's future.

"Too many years!" she said with a laugh. "You going to try?"

"No, thanks. I'm not feeling lucky tonight."

"Is something wrong? You look awful."

"Too much food," I said, pushing away the cake. "Let's get going."

As we walked out of the coffee shop into the main lobby, I got a real surprise. Standing at a telephone was the same woman who'd followed us at Universal City.

Grabbing Serena's arm, I quickly led her away from the woman. "There she is again! We've got to do something, Serena."

She laughed. "You're too suspicious, Liz. Come on, let's go find the Toad."

She wouldn't have laughed if I'd told her about the apple pips predicting bad luck. I took a final look at the woman and crossed my fingers for luck as we left the main lobby. *Relax*, I told myself, but I just couldn't forget the way that woman kept turning up. Something was definitely wrong.

The Bonita Tower, where the Toad was staying, was a long way from the coffee shop, but it was a nice walk through the warm night air. Way above us people were standing on balconies, looking down at the emerald waters of an Olympic pool lit by underwater lights.

"Disneyland tomorrow!" I exclaimed. "I can't wait to see everything. Why don't you come with us?"

"I'd love to, Liz, but I'm supposed to be going with Papa and Señora Garcia and the Toad."

"How about spending some time with them, and some with me?"

"That sounds nice."

Outside the entrance to the Bonita Tower were some horse-shoe falls which churned and bubbled as they dropped down over rocks to pools full of koifish. I was leaning over a railing with Serena, looking down at the big fish with their golden markings, when Señora Garcia came out of the tower.

"Hello girls!" she said. "This is very useful, finding you here. I've just been called to the main lobby on an urgent matter, and I've had to leave Ramón alone in our rooms. Can you look after him until I get back?"

What a break! Ramón, a.k.a. the Toad, was falling right into our hands like an over-ripe kumquat. As Señora Garcia gave Serena her door key, I kept the itching powder hidden behind my back and tried to contain my excitement. The Toad would never know what hit him.

"Let's go!" Serena said, heading for the tower's front door which slid open like magic as we approached. A few people sat around in comfy-looking stuffed chairs, and I studied their faces as we waited for the elevator.

"What's taking it so long?" I said at last. "Is it stuck between floors?"

Eventually the doors opened and a whole herd of people poured out wearing name-tags and talking excitedly. As we rose up to the eighth floor, Serena talked about hotels she's stayed in where they give you free gifts like little sachets of shampoo, and chocolates are left on your pillow when the sheets are turned down at night. Right away it became my ambition to stay in a hotel where chocolates materialize in your room!

Approaching the suite we discussed strategy. Should we rush the Toad and bury him in itching powder, or do something more subtle so that Serena wouldn't get into trouble with Señora Garcia? Finally we decided that Serena would keep the Toad concentrating on his favourite program on the idiot box while I slipped into the bedroom and sprinkled the deadly powder inside his clothes.

But we were really disappointed when Serena unlocked the door. The Toad was gone. We called his name sweetly and looked under the beds, but there was no sign of the little creep.

"The TV's still on," I said. "He can't be far away."

"Señora Garcia is going to be furious. Ramón must have slipped away as soon as she left."

"There's his key on the table, so how's he planning to get back into the room? I wonder if something's happened to him?"

"Maybe he drowned in the toilet."

"Wouldn't that be nice?"

I'd lost interest in the itching powder so we headed for the elevator. We talked and joked, but I felt strange about the Toad's disappearance. Where had he gone? Why had he left his key behind? Some sixth sense told me there was a connection between the Toad's empty room and the apple pips predicting bad luck for Serena.

When we reached the main lobby, I couldn't believe what I saw. Señora Garcia was sitting in a chair, talking to the woman who'd been following us.

"Now do you believe me, Serena?"

For the first time I saw doubt in her eyes. "Maybe you're right, Liz. What should we do?"

"We'd better tell Señora Garcia, but I don't think we should interrupt them now."

I couldn't tell what they were talking about, because they were speaking Spanish, but the young woman was crying. Then she suddenly looked at her watch, stood up, and left.

This obviously surprised Señora Garcia, who shook her head as she came over to us. "What a strange woman! She called me to the lobby because she's from La Luceña and said she has a big problem. Then she cried and talked nonsense while she kept looking at her watch. Now she's gone, without even saying goodbye."

"Did you know her before?" I asked.

"No."

"Then how did she know you're on vacation at this hotel?"

Señora Garcia frowned. "That's a good question. By the way, what are you doing here? Is Ramón with you?"

Serena shook her head. "No. When we got to your suite, Ramón wasn't there."

"Not there?" Señora Garcia sounded tense. "Was he hiding? Did you look for him? He loves to play tricks on me."

"We looked everywhere for him. He must have left the suite, but he didn't take his key."

"Ramón wouldn't do something like that!"

Her voice had become really high-pitched, and I realized how important the Toad was to Señora Garcia. I was glad that we hadn't pulled our stunt with the itching powder, but I was still very worried. Quickly I told her about being followed at Universal City, and suggested that the woman might have something to do with Ramón's disappearance.

"Don't call it a disappearance," Señora Garcia said, with a nervous smile. "I'm sure it's just one of his tricks. When I return to the suite, Ramón will rush out from a special hiding place. He's so sweet."

"Shouldn't we call the police?"

"Of course not."

"What if Ramón isn't in the room?"

"Then I *may* call the authorities."

"We'd better come with you, to help."

"What nonsense," Señora Garcia snapped, then walked quickly away. Serena shook her head.

"I apologize for her rudeness, Liz. She's just worried about Ramón."

"It doesn't matter, Serena. I guess I'd better get a taxi back to my motel."

Then two more strange things happened.

As we walked to the parking lot, a car came shooting out from behind the hotel, swerved onto West Street and was gone. I'm not sure if the little dark-haired person I caught sight of in the car was the Toad, but I sure recognized the beautiful woman in the back seat.

About two minutes later, after Serena had left to tell Señora Garcia about the car, a taxi came off West Street and threaded its way through the parking lot. When the driver was close enough to see me, a look of surprise crossed his face. Then he hit the accelerator and the taxi went squealing away.

I was just as shocked as the driver. I'd recognized him. It was Kingsley.

4

I decided not to tell Aunt Melody about seeing Kingsley at the wheel of the taxi.

It would only have made her more suspicious of him, and I was still sort of hoping they'd get together. Besides, there was probably a good explanation, like maybe Kingsley was going to star in a movie about cab drivers and was researching the part.

But then why go flying out of the parking lot when he saw me? The whole thing was totally confusing, and I didn't want to think that there might be a connection between Kingsley's weird behaviour and the Toad disappearing from his room. Maybe, I hoped, there'd be a chance to question Kingsley during our visit to Disneyland.

In the morning, after putting on my best jeans and a t-shirt with a big maple-leaf flag, I tried to phone Serena about the

Toad but there was no answer. Minutes later Kingsley arrived and the excitement of *finally* going to Disneyland made me forget all about the little creep.

As we walked to Disneyland I could see the famous white mountain, the Matterhorn, rising above the walls, but the only other sight was a huge parking lot that could probably qualify for the Guinness Book of Records. Sunlight sparkled off thousands of cars and shone on the mobs of people hurrying toward a row of ticket booths.

I raced ahead across the parking lot, hoping Aunt Melody and Kingsley would take the hint and move faster. Stopping to wait for them, I watched the monorail whistle past like a silver bullet in the sunshine. Some passengers waved down to me and then they were gone, heading for the station inside the Disneyland walls.

"What are you staring at, Liz?" Kingsley said, laughing. "Never seen a monorail before?"

I smiled. "They're pretty thin on the ground in Winnipeg. I wish they'd build one direct from my house to Queenston School. It would sure beat struggling through a blizzard in January."

Kingsley offered to treat us to tickets, but Aunt Melody insisted on buying ours. We each received a little booklet containing coupons for different attractions, plus a map of Disneyland showing how it's divided into seven different theme areas like Tomorrowland, with a bunch of space-age rides, and Adventureland, which features a Jungle Cruise and the Swiss Family Robinson Treehouse.

"I can't make up my mind! I want to go everywhere, *right now*!"

Kingsley smiled. "Bear Country is my favourite, but little kids usually like Fantasyland best. Want to go there?"

That really bothered me, and I didn't hide it. "I wish you wouldn't think of me as a little kid. I've been through a lot in my time, you know. Let me tell you sometime about the night a loony tried to bump off my brother and me at Lunenburg."

Kingsley put his arm around me. "You misunderstood me, Liz. I just thought you'd enjoy watching the kids riding the teacups and zooming around in special little racing cars. Melody tells me you're very fond of children."

"Can I believe you?" I asked, wanting to trust him, but fighting against being sucked in by his good looks and that strong arm hugging my shoulders.

"Of course."

"Then would you tell me something, Kingsley?"

"Sure."

Leaning close, so Aunt Melody wouldn't hear, I whispered, "Didn't I see you driving a cab last night?"

Kingsley hesitated for just a moment, and that was enough for me to know the answer. As he struggled for words, I smiled. "I don't *care*, you know. But I wish you'd trust me enough to be honest."

Those blue eyes looked right into me, making something flutter in my tummy. I braced myself, trying to resist Kingsley's charm, and then Aunt Melody broke in.

"Come on, you two! We've got lots to see."

Kingsley squeezed my shoulders, then walked over to her. So now I knew that he had been driving that cab, but I was no closer to the reason why. Probably I was actually further from the truth, because Kingsley would now be on his guard. Shaking my head, I followed them through the gate.

"No metal detectors?" I asked the man who took my ticket.

"What?"

"Aren't you afraid of people sneaking in weapons?"

Laughing, he looked at my maple-leaf t-shirt. "You Canadians sure are paranoid! Have a nice day in the Kingdom of the Mouse."

"Not paranoid, just careful," I replied, but he was already

telling someone else to have a nice day. I shrugged, and took my first look at Disneyland.

In front of me was an old-fashioned brick railway station with gingerbread gables and an American flag rippling against the blue sky. A steam engine came hissing into the station with its brass bell clanging, and right away I wanted to ride it.

On the sloping lawn in front of the station was the face of Mickey Mouse, made entirely of red and white flowers. All kinds of tourists were having their pictures taken beside Mickey's face, and there was even a Japanese guy shooting the scene with a portable video camera. I watched the engine go puffing and clanging out of the station, pulling a load of open cars jammed with passengers, then ran to Aunt Melody.

"Let's take the train first! On the map it goes all around the outside of Disneyland, so we'll see everything."

"Okay, but how do we get to that station?"

Kingsley took her hand, and I noticed she didn't let go. "We follow this tunnel under the tracks, then climb the station stairs on the other side."

Running ahead through the tunnel, I stopped to stare in amazement. In front of me was a perfect little town right out of the past. There was even a band dressed in red uniforms and playing oom-pah music as it marched around a leafy square crowded with adults and kids who were clapping in time with the big bass drum. I go for any kind of music, so I stood watching the band until it had disappeared down a street of cream-coloured stores.

Except they weren't called stores at all. One was an *emporium*, another was a *cinema*, and a third was a *penny arcade*. Their signs were outlined with light bulbs, not neon, and all along the street were gas lamps and graceful old trees, their green leaves shimmering in the sun. I'd walked straight into the past!

"Let's go explore, Aunt Melody," I said, as she approached.

"I'm dying to sample that ice cream parlour with the frilly yellow curtains in the window."

"What about the train ride?"

"I couldn't sit still long enough! I just want to see it all. I feel so good, like it's my birthday or something."

Behind me I heard a *clippity-clop,* and turned to see a horse with a silver mane pulling an open streetcar full of tourists clicking away with their cameras. Then the streetcar stopped, and Goofy jumped off! I couldn't believe it, especially when he came straight over to me and stuck out his white-gloved hand.

"Hi, there," he said in that crazy voice. "My name is Goofy and I'm in love with you."

I laughed, then tried to think of something clever to say, but I was too embarrassed because everyone was staring. Goofy lifted his hat to me, then went charging into the square and slid along a park bench doing the splits.

"He's showing off," Aunt Melody said. "You bring out the worst in these men, Liz."

I just smiled, and wished I hadn't left my camera in the motel room. Nobody back home would believe I'd met Goofy in person.

"Let's get *going,* Aunt Melody!"

"Listen, sweetie, why not explore by yourself? We won't be able to keep up with you."

So she wanted to be alone with Kingsley! Smiling to myself, I arranged to meet them at Sleeping Beauty's Castle before lunch, then I blasted off. Probably I should have stuck close to Kingsley so I could grill him about the Curious Incident of the Cab in the Night, but I was too excited to concentrate on detecting. Lots of time later, I told myself, because it looked like he'd be around for some time.

I headed for the penny arcade which had a collection of totally ancient pinball machines that our poor old forefathers were stuck with playing in the days before video games. Then I spotted a mechanical gypsy named Esmeralda who dispensed my fortune on a printed card for only a penny. *Beware of handsome strangers,* it read. *Black deeds lurk in the hearts of men.*

I shuddered, then flipped the card into a litter bin, wondering if Kingsley qualified as a stranger, or if he was now a friend. And if not Kingsley, who was the handsome man with black deeds lurking in his heart? Darn old Esmeralda, I thought. Now she's ruined my day.

It took a few minutes to get back into the Disneyland spirit, but the sun warmed me up as I stopped to check my map and my watch. I was due to meet Serena at eleven, so there was just time to explore Disneyland's Haunted Mansion. To get there I had to pass through New Orleans Square where shuttered houses stood close together on narrow streets, and wisteria blossoms spilled down from iron-lace balconies. I listened to a jazz combo wearing straw boaters and checked jackets, and then stared in the window of a tiny shop at a pirate galleon of pure white blown glass, with coloured flags streaming from its masts. I couldn't begin to afford the galleon, but I did spot a little figurine of Goofy, a perfect souvenir.

The Haunted Mansion was an old southern place that stood alone among the trees, its dark windows watching suspiciously as I approached, trying not to notice the graveyard. I'm normally fairly brave, but there's something about ghosts and vampires that gets to me, and I felt just a wee bit nervous as I stepped inside.

Other visitors had already gathered in a shadowed room under a chandelier. We waited and waited while our nerves stretched tight. Then a door suddenly opened and everyone screamed!

But it was only a false alarm, and we all tiptoed into a second room where a ghostly voice warned, "It's too late to turn back." When the floor began to sink I *really* screamed, but then I had to laugh because the pictures on the wall were being stretched and one stuffy-looking man in a portrait slowly lost his trousers, revealing his striped boxer shorts.

In an underground passage we climbed into little carriages called "doom buggies" and rode past some really spooky scenes. In one room covered with cobwebs, a banquet was in progress and wispy ghosts were dancing right through the tables and chairs. A few minutes later, after going past an indoor grave-yard, we came to a dimly lit mirror. When I looked in it I saw a ghost riding beside me in the doom buggy. Even though I knew it was only a clever special effect, I was still pretty glad to see sunshine again.

It was also great to see Serena waiting outside the Golden Horseshoe Saloon where we'd arranged to meet. But there was something wrong. She was standing in the shadows of the saloon, and only poked her head out to attract my attention before ducking back into hiding.

"What's wrong, Serena?"

"It's that woman! She's following me again."

"Not the same one from yesterday?"

"Yes! I saw her a half-hour ago, following me through the crowd. I pretended not to notice, and led her inside the saloon. A few minutes ago I snuck away."

"Is she still in there?"

Serena nodded. "I've been watching the door while I waited for you. She thinks I'm in the washroom, but it's got a side door she doesn't know about."

"We'd better get your dad. Where is he?"

Serena made a helpless gesture. "Somewhere in Disney-land. But I'm meeting him and Señora Garcia later for lunch."

"I wonder what that woman is after? Hey, I almost forgot. What about the Toad? Did he show up last night?"

"It was strange because . . . " Serena grabbed my arm and squeezed tight. "There she is!"

Whirling around, I saw the woman standing in front of the

saloon, wearing the same wrinkled blouse and faded jeans. Today, though, two things were different about her. She was carrying a leather attache case, and she looked very worried.

For a few minutes she carefully studied the crowd. After that she looked at her watch, and then scanned the crowd again.

"She's looking for you, Serena," I whispered. "But why?"

The woman walked toward a small river which curved through this part of Disneyland. I was almost afraid to follow her, in spite of the fact that we were surrounded by thousands of people. Then I squeezed Serena's arm.

"Let's see where she's going."

The woman paused at the river's edge to watch a bunch of kids paddle by in a war canoe, then sat down on a bench with the attache case in her lap. A man was sitting at the other end of the bench, also holding an attache case. She leaned toward him and they started talking.

Suddenly the man slammed his fist against the bench and walked angrily away. The woman went after him and we followed close behind.

The pair headed toward a nearby pier where a stern-wheeler, the *Mark Twain*, was preparing to set sail. Steam rose from the tall stacks and a brass bell clanged as the last tourists crowded onto the open decks and the captain signalled to throw off the mooring lines.

"They're getting on board! Find an admission coupon fast, Serena."

We raced through the gate, shoving our coupons at the surprised attendant, and scrambled aboard the *Mark Twain* as the whistle blew. There was a slight lurch, then I heard the sound of waves slapping the hull as the sternwheeler started moving.

Going to the railing, I took a quick look at the thick woods on the far shore, then spotted the woman and her companion in the sunshine on the open bow, talking together.

"Wait here, Serena, so she doesn't see you. I'm going to sit behind them and try to hear what they're saying."

"Isn't that taking a chance?"

I smiled. "If they throw me overboard, it's a short swim to shore." Giving Serena the thumbs-up sign, I walked boldly forward and dropped into a seat directly behind the pair. As I expected, they were too busy with their conversation to notice me, and I had my first close-up look at the man.

To put it briefly, on a scale of 10 he scored at least a 12. He had an athlete's body and was beautifully dressed in an expensive shirt and tailored slacks. His shirt cuffs were rolled back, revealing a heavy gold chain on his wrist, and a deep tan. Best of all was his wavy brown hair, the kind you want to run your fingers through.

There was only one thing wrong about this man. His eyes were terrifying.

I've seen dangerous people before, but nothing has ever frightened me quite like those pale blue eyes.

It was like there was no soul in them.

I almost walked away, I was so upset. Then, taking a deep breath, I leaned closer to the man, trying to hear his conversation. At first I couldn't make out the words, but then he turned to face the woman directly. "Since you've failed, we must count on G. If that doesn't work, there'll be other kids. Now let's review our plans one last time."

Walking to the railing, he pointed into the woods. As I moved closer, trying to hear, I saw a log fort appear among the trees. The tall stockades were straight out of an old cowboy movie, and there were even blockhouses at each corner of the fort, with rifle ports and long barrels poking out into the sunshine. It was so realistic that I stared until it was out of sight, and when I looked again for the man and woman they were gone.

I raced off in search of them and with Serena's help finally found them on the top deck alone at the stern. Unable to get close, I told Serena what I'd heard and waited to see what they'd do next. For a while they were silent, but then the man said something and pointed into the woods.

"There's that fort again, Serena." Getting out my map, I found it on a small island. "It's called Fort Wilderness, and it's on Tom Sawyer Island. I wonder why that gruesome twosome is so interested in a fort?"

Serena sighed. "I'm getting bored, Liz. Let's forget about them."

I stared at her in surprise. "How can you say that? Maybe we've stumbled onto a major plot."

She laughed. "Being at Disneyland is making your imagination run wild, Liz. You've got to stop playing games."

"What do you mean, games? You were pretty frightened back at the saloon."

"Sure, but I've changed my mind. Obviously the woman's just in love, and I think we should leave them alone." Without another word, Serena headed down the stairs to the lower deck.

"Hey, Serena, come back! What if . . . !"

But she was gone, and I was left alone feeling like a fool. For a few more minutes I watched the couple at the stern, hoping they'd do something monstrous that would prove I'd been right, then I followed Serena below.

"Maybe you're right," I said, as the sternwheeler approached the pier with its brass bell clanging. "There's no sense wasting my precious time at Disneyland following around two strangers."

"It's pure coincidence seeing that woman two days running. Forget her Liz."

I nodded, trying to believe Serena was right. After all, I was on holiday, so why worry about some woman who kept turning up like a bad penny? Besides, her friend scared me, and I wanted to steer clear of him.

"How about a ride on Big Thunder Mountain?" Serena suggested. "It's my favourite."

"Sounds good."

At first I couldn't forget the mysterious couple, but then a crazy ride on a runaway mining train drove them out of my head. Actually, at first the ride on Big Thunder Mountain seemed pretty tame because the train just rattled along past some tall rock buttes and through a gold rush town, but then the train entered a pitch-black railway tunnel and people started hollering when they saw bats' eyes glowing all around.

Those eyes didn't bother me, but I couldn't help screaming when the train speeded up, then started twisting and plunging through the darkness. We rushed out into daylight just long enough to pass a mountain goat chewing a stick of dynamite, then swung wildly around a corner and went flying straight into a mining tunnel with a ceiling so low I thought my head would be torn off. I panicked and ducked, but at the last second the whole train dropped into darkness and we flew through another series of blind twists and turns.

By the time it was over I was drenched in sweat and my voice was hoarse from screaming. "Fabulous!" I croaked to Serena. "Let's go again."

She shook her head. "I have to meet Papa and Señora Garcia at the Cafe Orleans for lunch. Please join us."

I looked at my watch. "I'm supposed to eat with Aunt Melody and Kingsley, but we're not meeting for an hour. I guess I could nibble a little something in the meantime."

As we walked toward New Orleans Square, I looked at Serena. "You never told me about the Toad. Did he show up?"

"Apparently, but I wasn't allowed to see him this morning."

"What happened?"

"I went to Señora Garcia's suite to ask about Ramón. She said he was feeling ill and wouldn't be going to Disneyland. I started to open his bedroom door to say goodbye, but Señora Garcia yanked me away."

"*Weird.* Did she say anything?"

"Just that Ramón was too sick to see anyone."

"How did she look? Upset?"

"Sure, but why wouldn't she be if Ramón is sick?"

I stopped walking, and looked carefully at Serena. "Tell me something. If her son is that sick, why is Señora Garcia visiting Disneyland today?"

Serena shrugged. "She wants to have a good time."

"You're wrong, Serena. There's something strange happening here and Señora Garcia is involved."

She smiled. "What an imagination you've got."

"Just listen to some facts. First, a woman follows us at Universal City. Second, the same woman is at the hotel when Ramón disappears from his room."

"But he came back."

"Did you actually see him?"

"No, but . . ."

"Third, Señora Garcia won't let you see the Toad this morning, then leaves for Disneyland. Notice that the Toad **is** left unprotected, even though there's just been a scare about him disappearing."

"So what? Don't tell me you think she's kidnapped her own son?"

"Of course not, but maybe he's being held hostage and she can't say anything because his life is threatened."

"Why would anyone want Ramón as a hostage? He'd have *them* begging for mercy!"

I had to admit the idea was pretty funny, but I was still feeling suspicious as we reached the Cafe Orleans and were shown to an outdoor table where a huge man with thick white hair sat beside Señora Garcia. Was she linked to the mysterious couple on the sternwheeler? I'd have given anything to know.

"Papa, this is my Canadian friend, Liz Austen."

His right side was disabled, but his left-handed grip was powerful.

"It's a great pleasure to meet you, Liz. I'm sorry I missed your performance at Castle Dracula."

"We had a great time, Señor Hernandez. Thanks a million for treating me to dinner last night."

"You're welcome. I believe you know Señora Garcia?"

"Sure," I said, sitting down beside her. "I'm sorry Ramón is sick."

"I'm sure he'll be fine!" she exclaimed, with a smile that would have taken top prize for Phoniest in the Show. She looked tired, and she was no longer the same aggressive woman I'd met yesterday.

"Now, Liz," Señor Hernandez said with his deep voice, "what do you want? You're my guest, so have anything."

My mouth literally watered as I studied the menu, discovering sodas and freezes. I tried to restrain myself, remembering I had to have lunch in an hour, but then I realized eating here would save Aunt Melody the expense.

"The Marquis Sandwich looks great, Señor Hernandez. Would that be okay?"

He smiled. "The sky's the limit."

After our order had been taken I turned to Serena. "Are you going to tell your dad about being followed?"

"Of course not," she said, laughing. "That was just my imagination."

Señor Hernandez frowned. "You were followed, precious?"

"Forget it, Papa. I was mistaken."

"Tell me exactly what happened." Now he looked upset, and I remembered that he'd lost his wife and other daughter to a terrorist bomb. The poor man was probably worried constantly about losing Serena.

When she said nothing, I realized the ball was in my court,

so I described everything that had happened. I even included Señora Garcia's meeting in the hotel lobby with the beautiful woman, and my suspicion that I'd seen the woman driving away with Ramón, but Señor Hernandez didn't seem particularly interested in those things.

Instead, he reached for Serena's hand. "You must stay with me until we leave Disneyland. These things worry me."

"What nonsense," Serena snapped, pulling free of his hand. "Don't baby me, Papa."

"Please, my precious. I implore you. Stay close to me."

"This is Disneyland, Papa. Nothing is going to happen here."

Señora Garcia shook her head. "You could be wrong, Serena. Please, do as your father asks, and stay with us. We're going to explore Frontierland this afternoon."

"Yes," Señor Hernandez said, nodding vigorously, "and later I shall buy souvenirs for you and Liz. Anything you want, from those exclusive shops in New Orleans Square that you like so much."

I confess my ears twitched, remembering that glass galleon with its coloured flags, so I was a little disappointed when Serena refused to discuss the matter further. As a result of her decision, which I considered pretty pig-headed, all of us ate in gloomy silence. When Serena and I stood up to leave, Señora Garcia touched her hand.

"A final time, Serena, I beg you to be nice. At least come with us now to Tom Sawyer Island, so we can enjoy a bit of your company. After that you and Liz can explore on your own."

I felt sorry for the adults, trying to get Serena to cooperate so they could relax and have some fun. "Let's do it, Serena!" I said. "I'd like to see Tom Sawyer Island, and then we can go try the Jungle Cruise."

As she hesitated, her father beamed at me. "Perhaps we can all go on the Jungle Cruise, and then do some shopping. Remember, the treat's on me!"

Serena sighed. "Oh ... very well."

Success! The rest of us grinned, and I felt like shaking hands all round. But then I remembered Aunt Melody.

"Hey, I'm supposed to meet my aunt and Kingsley. Can Serena come with me to find them?"

Señora Garcia looked at her watch. "Perhaps Serena should stay with us, and Liz can join us later today with her aunt."

Serena shook her head. "I'm sticking with Liz."

"But ..."

"I mean it!"

"Really, Serena, you ..."

Good grief! It took forever to reach an agreement, but finally Serena and I arranged to meet the others in 15 minutes, and went off to find Aunt Melody and Kingsley. As soon as we'd left the cafe, Serena sighed and shook her head.

"Papa, Papa, Papa! I love him dearly, but he is so protective that I just go crazy."

"Can I ask something personal? What caused his disability?"

"He had a stroke shortly after my mother and sister were killed. Everyone wanted him to quit working, but he refused. His job is all he's got left."

"Plus you, Serena. I guess he's over-protective because he's afraid of losing you."

She nodded. "And as a result, I'm spoiled rotten. I can have anything I want, but even that gets boring."

I remembered the glass galleon. "Will he really take us shopping this afternoon?"

"Of course, Liz, and you must choose a very nice souvenir. I might get something for my villa."

"Your *what*?"

"Papa has bought me a villa on the Pacific Coast in La Luceña. It's my wedding present."

"What! Are you engaged?"

"Of course not," Serena said, laughing. "But the villa will be mine the moment I marry."

"Aren't you planning to do anything else, like travel or have a career?"

Serena lifted her shoulders in an elegant shrug. "Why bother? Those things don't interest me."

We met Aunt Melody and Kingsley outside Sleeping Beauty's Castle. Fortunately they'd been nibbling goodies all morning so they didn't want any lunch, and quickly agreed to visit Tom Sawyer Island.

"Fort Wilderness is great," Kingsley said. "It's so authentic, you almost expect to be attacked and see arrows whizzing over the walls."

I wondered if it was just a coincidence that Kingsley had mentioned Fort Wilderness so soon after it was discussed by the couple on the sternwheeler. Then I shook my head, trying to stop my imagination from running away, and made myself chat to Kingsley about the history of Disneyland as we walked to the river where rafts would take us across to Tom Sawyer Island.

Señora Garcia was waiting by the water. Even from a distance I could see she was a bundle of nerves, pacing along the river bank as she stared at her watch. When she saw us she ran to Serena.

"Where have you been? You took longer than 15 minutes."

"That's not true. Don't be rude to me, Señora Garcia, or we'll leave."

Señora Garcia held up both hands. "I'm sorry, Serena. Please, let's hurry. Your father is waiting at the rafts."

"Don't you want to meet Liz's aunt, and Kingsley?"

"Of course!"

Looking really flustered, Señora Garcia introduced herself, then hustled us all to the pier. Within minutes we had made the short trip across to the island and were following a dirt trail in the direction of Fort Wilderness. Señor Hernandez walked very slowly, leaning heavily on his cane, and I hung back to chat with him.

"You know what was here before Disneyland?"

"No I don't, Liz. Tell me."

"Just a bunch of orange groves. Can you believe how perfectly they've been turned into this Mississippi River island? There are even real ducks paddling through the reeds. Walt Disney was a genius!"

He laughed. "I like you very much, Liz, and I am glad that Serena is your friend. She has some rough edges, but perhaps they will be softened by your influence."

"She's a nice person, Señor Hernandez. Maybe she'll have a chance to visit me in Winnipeg."

"Yes," he said, nodding thoughtfully. "How fortunate you are to have a peaceful country, Liz. All my life I have yearned for such peace for the people of La Luceña, but it has not come to pass."

I tried to think of something to say, but how can you comfort a man who has been through so much? I felt so sad watching him struggle along this path with sweat running down his face, wearing himself out just to be near his daughter.

"I'm sure Serena will be okay, Señor Hernandez. It was just a fluke seeing that woman both days."

"Thank you, Liz. You are kind to say so."

At last we reached the fort where people swarmed in and out through the open gate. All these tourists in t-shirts and jeans sure didn't resemble the Old West, but a security guard dressed as a cavalry officer made the scene a little more authentic, and there were some terrific displays of artifacts inside a couple of small log buildings located within the fort.

One building which had a sign reading *Regimental Headquarters* showed U.S. Army officers on the frontier with their buckskin coats and muskets. To me, though, the second building was more interesting because the displays showed things people used every day like home-made candles and birchbark pails.

Besides which, there was a canteen! Deciding I had a little

room left in my tummy, I bought a brownie and some lemonade, and wandered out into the sunshine to find a bench where I could rest my feet.

But I never made it. Standing across the yard of the fort was the beautiful dark-haired woman and, at her side, the man with the cruel eyes. In their hands were submachine guns.

5

I couldn't believe my eyes.

The woman walked slowly toward a corner of the yard where a group of tourists huddled together with their arms around each other. Standing guard over them was a man with a submachine gun.

My eyes jumped to another corner where a woman with a gun was threatening a second group of terrified people. Among them were Aunt Melody and Kingsley, clinging to each other.

My hands were shaking so much that I dropped my food. I wondered foolishly if I should clean up the mess, then looked again at Aunt Melody. She was pointing toward the open gate.

"Run, Liz!"

But I was frozen, and could only stare at the people who were racing out of the gate. As they ran to safety a young man and woman with guns strapped over their shoulders were pulling the gate closed, and within seconds it was bolted shut. I'd lost my chance.

I ran to hug Aunt Melody.

"Are they going to kill us?"

"Sssh, darling," she said, holding me tight. "It's going to be okay."

"I told you that woman was following us for a reason! Who is she? Why are they doing this?"

"We'll know soon. Try to be quiet."

Serena and her father were nearby gripping each other's hands, and Señora Garcia leaned against the fort's log wall with tears running from her eyes. Other people just stared at the guns and the cold faces of the young people holding them. Then suddenly a woman from the crowd pushed past me and walked with a determined face to the middle of the yard.

"I demand to be released," she said to the man with the cruel eyes. "If not, I have powerful friends in the government who will have you arrested."

The man just stared at her.

"I won't tell you again!" she shouted in his face. "Release me this minute."

With a swift movement the man slapped her. The woman spun backwards and fell face down, the contents of her purse scattering across the yard. She struggled up to her hands and knees but the man reached forward with his foot and sent her sprawling again. Then he took a pistol from his belt and aimed it at the woman. Slowly he pulled the trigger.

With a pitiful gesture the woman held up her hands to stop the bullet. When nothing happened the man squeezed the trigger again, laughing, and I realized the safety catch was on. Then he pointed it at our small group huddled by the wall.

"You are prisoners of war," he said in a voice that was pitched high by excitement. "My name is the Dragon. You must obey my every command or face death. You have been captured by the November 24th Movement which seeks freedom for the people of La Luceña. You will be released unharmed if the government of La Luceña meets my demands. If not, you will die."

I trembled as I held Aunt Melody. Then I heard the sound of feet as a teenaged boy raced in a blind panic toward the gate of the fort. Reaching it, he struggled desperately to unlock the heavy bolts while the terrorists watched without making a move to stop him.

At last, as the boy managed to get one bolt loose, the Dragon signalled to a man holding a weapon that had a thick black barrel. He raised it, and fired. There was a loud WHUMP as the boy was hit and went down, then the Dragon laughed.

"He has been knocked out by a stun gun, so he will live. The next person who tries to escape will die."

Serena's father, who had been sitting on a bench, pulled himself up and limped forward on his cane. "I am the consul for La Luceña. Have you taken these hostages because I am here today?"

The Dragon nodded, but said nothing.

"Let these people go and keep me as your hostage."

"Not a chance, Consul. The police will arrive soon and they'll be forced to bargain because I hold prisoners. If the government of La Luceña doesn't meet my demands I will begin killing hostages one by one."

"At least free the children!"

The Dragon laughed. "The children are my strength. While we hold them the police will be powerless to attack, which is why I chose Disneyland to take prisoners. Soon my face will be on television everywhere, as people wait to know if I will let the Disneyland children live or die."

"You are sadistic, and stupid."

For the first time I saw an emotion in the Dragon's eyes. Anger. He aimed his submachine gun at Serena's father and released the safety catch. "Don't push me, Consul. If I kill you I can still use your daughter for bargaining with the La Luceña government."

At his signal, terrorists walked toward us. For a moment I thought they were choosing victims, but instead we were ordered to hand over our valuables and wallets. A woman pleaded to keep her family snapshots but was refused, and they even made us take off our shoes, which seemed crazy to me.

"Do exactly what they say," Aunt Melody ordered. "If we want to leave here alive, we mustn't make them angry."

"But why take our shoes and that woman's pictures?"

"So we'll feel less like people. It gives them an advantage."

One of the terrorists reached for Kingsley's gold chain and savagely tore it away from his neck. Kingsley gasped with pain, and for a second I thought he would hit the terrorist, but nothing happened. A fat man who had started crying when his platinum watch was removed offered to pay cash for his release but the terrorists ignored him. There were six of them, only teenagers, but they moved among us like robots. One of them didn't even notice when one of the hostages gave him a warm smile. She was wearing short-shorts and a yellow halter-top, and I felt sick when I saw her smile at the terrorist. Some people are insane.

"You!" the Dragon snapped, pointing at a middle-aged blond in a khaki outfit. "Step forward."

With a terrified face the woman left our group. She took a few steps toward the Dragon, then stopped and hugged her arm across her stomach. She had a rose tattooed on her upper arm, and sweat had streaked the mascara around her eyes. She looked pathetic, and I felt terribly sorry for her.

"Are you afraid of me?" the Dragon demanded.

"Yes," the woman answered in a tiny voice.

"Yes, what?"

"Yes, sir."

"Approach me."

The woman took a step, then her legs gave out and she fell to her knees. Terrorists dragged her forward and she knelt in front of the Dragon as her tears fell in big drops to the ground.

The security guard dressed as a cavalry officer was then ordered forward, followed by the woman who'd wanted to save her family pictures and a bearded man wearing a *Harley-Davidson* t-shirt. As the Dragon's eyes swept over the remaining hostages my heart pounded because I thought that the next adult he chose would be Aunt Melody, but somehow she was spared as several more men and women were told to step forward.

Surrounded by guns, the group was marched slowly across the yard. The bearded man made a half-hearted attempt to break free, but he was knocked back by a muscular terrorist.

The group was ordered to halt beside the gate. A terrorist slid back the heavy bolts and then, to my complete astonishment, all of the hostages were pushed through the gate and we saw them staggering, walking and running to the freedom of the woods. Seconds later the gate was slammed shut, and I looked in astonishment at Aunt Melody.

"What happened? Why did the Dragon let them go?"

"He was getting rid of excess baggage."

"What do you mean?"

"There were too many hostages to be guarded by only six people. As he said, all he really needs are children."

"We've got to escape! There must be a way out."

Squeezing me tighter, Aunt Melody shook her head. "If you're caught trying to escape, you'll be shot. A man like that wouldn't hesitate to make an example of you."

"But I'm only a kid!"

She nodded. "If he starts killing the children, the authorities will do anything he says. That's his strength, and he knows it."

Kingsley patted my hand. "Listen to your aunt, Liz. She's right."

"How do you think they got those submachine guns through Disneyland without anyone seeing?"

"There's your answer." Kingsley pointed at some attaché cases lying in a dusty corner of the yard. "While you were inside looking at the displays, I saw these people come into the fort carrying attaché cases. Before I could say anything to your aunt they'd opened the cases and taken out the guns. It happened so fast we didn't have a chance."

"But where did they come from?"

"They'd probably been hiding in the woods."

"But *why*? Are they going to steal our money?"

"I doubt if it's as simple as that, Liz."

Suddenly I remembered Kingsley's strange behaviour and the fact that he'd mentioned this fort just after I'd seen the terrorists discussing it. Was there a link? As I studied his face, trying to find the truth, he smiled and I felt a rush of guilt.

"Oh, Kingsley, I *know* you're not one of these terrorists!"

Despite the guns threatening us, he laughed out loud. "Me, a terrorist? What gave you that idea?"

I blushed. "Blame my overactive imagination." I hesitated, wondering if I should ask him about the taxi, but then Aunt Melody put a finger to her lips.

"Try not to talk too much, Liz, or it will attract that man's attention. He's more dangerous than you may realize."

"Have you heard of him before?"

She nodded. "He hires himself out to revolutionary groups and leads their terrorist operations in return for huge payments. Obviously these people from La Luceña hired the Dragon to be their leader."

"But what do they want?"

"I'm sure we'll find out soon. No doubt they picked Disneyland for the publicity that they would get."

As we spoke, the Dragon directed four terrorists to climb to the parapets. These wooden walks, which were near the top of the stockade walls, allowed them to look down at the woods and watch for the arrival of the police. They reminded me of the people who once defended these forts on the frontier, except now it was the rescuers who would be kept out.

The two remaining terrorists herded us together in a small group and stood guard with their guns. One of them seemed to get a kick out of clicking her gun's trigger and watching people wince, but the other watched us silently without showing any emotion.

Señora Garcia was still sobbing. It was such a sad sound that I was pleased when Serena went over and put an arm around her shoulders.

"It's all my fault," Señora Garcia sobbed. "I led you into this trap."

"Don't be silly," Serena said gently. "We all wanted to visit the fort."

"But you don't understand, Serena. I made you and your father come this afternoon so you'd be here when the terrorists seized the fort."

"What do you mean?"

"Liz was right. She did see Ramón being driven away last night. That woman used a false story to get me down to the lobby so the others could kidnap Ramón. They threatened to kill him if I called the police."

"But why did they want Ramón?"

"Don't you see? They needed my help to get you to this fort. But I should never have done it! Now we're all prisoners, and they'll probably still kill Ramón."

"Of course they won't. Don't you worry, he's going to be fine."

I really admired Serena for the way she continued to comfort this woman who had betrayed her. Her father was great, too, because he reached out to Señora Garcia and held her hand. In fact both of them were behaving a lot better than me. I was furious to think that the rest of us were in this terrible danger because of Señora Garcia.

"She should never have done it," I whispered to Aunt Melody. "We could all be killed just because of that little brat of hers."

"When you're a mother, Liz, you'll understand."

"If I produce a child like the Toad, you can banish me to Tuktoyaktuk."

She smiled. "Not much chance of that."

"Aunt Melody, why do you think that woman followed us? Do you think they were planning to kidnap Serena earlier today?"

Aunt Melody shook her head. "I'm sure they were counting on Señora Garcia to get her here."

"Why grab Serena?"

"Probably because her father is the consul. By threatening his daughter's life, they may force the La Luceña government to give in to their demands. He has . . ."

Just then there was a warning cry from the parapet, and the air was blasted by the huge rotors of a helicopter which roared in above the wall and hovered over the fort, shaking us with the force of the wind storm it created. Painted on the orange belly was A.T.A.C., and I glimpsed a face looking down at us from a plexiglass bubble in the helicopter's nose.

"This is the police!" a voice said from a speaker. "Throw down your weapons and leave the fort peacefully."

I looked at the Dragon, alone in the centre of the yard. His hair was being tossed wildly by the wind, but he managed to stand firm. Raising his submachine gun, he fired. The plexiglass bubble shattered and immediately the helicopter lifted straight into the sky. It angled to the side and was lost from sight.

"You cowards!" the Dragon screamed. "Come back and fight!"

Grinning, he looked around at the terrorists for approval.

One of them, the beautiful woman I'd seen following us, smiled at him but the others remained solemn. It was then I realized that they were as scared as the rest of us. Every person in the fort depended on the Dragon to get out of this trap.

"Mommy," a little girl said, "I want to go now."

"Sssh," her mother whispered.

"But I'm tired of the fort. Can't we ride Big Thunder Mountain now?"

My own ride on the runaway mining train seemed like a century ago, and I could hardly believe that Disneyland even existed. What was happening out there? Were people still enjoying themselves? Even though I could see the blue sky above, I felt suffocated.

"Police approaching through the woods!" a terrorist yelled from the parapet. "Should I shoot?"

The Dragon laughed. "Only when you see the whites of their eyes."

Seconds later a voice boomed from a speaker outside the fort. "Release all non-political hostages. We will then negotiate your demands."

The Dragon looked up at the parapet over the main gate. "Can you see them?" he asked the man stationed there.

"Yes. There are many police with guns, in the woods. I can see others across the river, all with weapons."

"What about television cameras?"

"Nothing."

"Tell the police that I, the Dragon, will decide when negotiations begin. No prisoners will be released. I must have hostages to kill if my demands are not met."

The terrorist leaned over the edge of the stockade and shouted this information to the police. The booming voice then offered to provide food in exchange for a hostage, but the Dragon turned this down. Silence followed, and I looked at Aunt Melody.

"Are the police going to attack the fort?" I whispered.

She shook her head. "That's too dangerous. They'll wait a long time, hoping to wear down the terrorists."

Serena looked at her with angry eyes. "Can't we do *anything* to get out of here?"

"Yes. We can stay calm."

"Big deal. Look, there are only seven of them. Why can't we rush them and grab their guns?"

"Because they're being very careful. That's one reason most of them are up on the parapets, away from us but ready to shoot. No, there's only one way we can help."

"What's that?"

"We can try to get to know them. If we can become individuals that they know and even care for, it will be much harder for them to kill us."

"I'm not talking to those rats!"

"That's fine, Serena, but just don't make them angry. Otherwise you'll probably be the first person chosen for execution."

For a moment Serena looked frightened. Then she shook her head and turned to study the terrorists. As she did, her fists clenched and unclenched.

"Don't do it, Serena," I whispered.

"Do what?"

"You're probably thinking of escaping, but it won't work. I didn't tell you at the time, but the apple pips predicted bad luck for you."

"Isn't this unlucky enough, being trapped here?"

"Maybe, but don't make it worse."

She tossed her black hair and turned away from me. There was nothing more I could say, so I looked at the other hostages to see if there was anyone who needed help. The kids looked fine, but two adults seemed to be taking it pretty hard.

The woman in short-shorts had moved away from the rest of us and was leaning against the log wall with a faraway look in her eyes that worried me. She seemed to have withdrawn into another world, but I was still disgusted at the way she had smiled at the terrorist and I decided to leave her alone.

Instead I crawled over to sit beside a white-haired woman who was the only person still sobbing. She was dressed neatly, in a white blouse and navy-blue skirt, so it seemed especially cruel that she was forced to go without shoes. Somehow it made her seem practically naked.

"It'll be okay," I said. "We'll be safe soon. The police will get us out."

This only seemed to upset the woman and she sobbed even harder.

"Please, talk to me. You've got an English accent. Are you on holiday?"

"Yes," she said, wiping her eyes. "This is my first visit to America. I came with my daughter and her husband. They were just released from the fort by that evil man. I may never see them again."

I squeezed her hand. "What's your name?"

"Mrs. Spencer."

"What's your favourite thing in Disneyland, Mrs. Spencer?"

Her eyes actually lit up when I said the magic word, Disneyland, and soon she was describing the beautiful gardens and all the music that she'd been enjoying. After that, as we talked about Universal City, other hostages began joining in and pretty soon we had a regular tea party going. People even laughed out loud when I described my horrible experience with the ear-plug at Castle Dracula, and for a time we were like close friends sitting in the sun enjoying the day.

As long as we didn't look at the guns.

6

For hours we watched the shadows grow behind the walls of the fort as evening approached. A balloon with Mickey Mouse ears had drifted across the sky, but there was no other sign that anyone now occupied Disneyland.

We were given food from the canteen, and were escorted to the fort's washrooms by the terrorists who remained completely silent. There wasn't a sign of the police and we saw little of the Dragon who issued orders to the terrorists from inside the small log building marked *Regimental Headquarters*.

I grew more and more tense as time passed and nothing happened. Some of the hostages who had been bitter and angry earlier now slumped against the wall staring into space, while a few kids played with a ball that someone had found in the canteen.

But there was one hostage I had grown to hate.

The young woman wearing the short-shorts seemed to be actually sympathetic to the terrorists. She had taken food up to the people patrolling the parapets and now stood in the door of the Regimental Headquarters flirting with the Dragon. I was too far away to hear their conversation, but I steamed when I saw her giggle and point in our direction.

"What's wrong with that woman?" I said to Aunt Melody. "Is she off her head?"

"She wants to live."

"Sure, but she doesn't have to put us down."

Kingsley patted my hand. "Ignore her, Liz. No sense upsetting your blood pressure."

"I'm going *crazy* with the waiting. Why doesn't something happen?"

Kingsley shook his head. "The police can't make a move in case someone gets hurt. And the Dragon isn't doing anything because it builds tension. As he predicted, people all over the world are probably glued to their TV sets, wondering what's going to happen. And just waiting . . ."

"It's just like torture, isn't it?"

"Yes, and I'm sure the Dragon is loving every minute of it. He obviously has an incredible need to be the centre of attention. You'd have thought, when the police arrived, that he'd have been worried. Instead he just asked if there were TV cameras outside."

I thought about my parents in Winnipeg, and what they would be going through. I tried to picture them puttering around our house on Campbell Avenue, but I knew that actually they'd be on the phone trying to get information, or just staring at the TV set.

A loud crackle came from the police speaker outside the fort, followed by a voice. "A radio reporter wants to enter the fort. Will you admit her?"

We all looked at the Regimental Headquarters and waited for the Dragon to appear. Like some kind of ham actor he kept us hanging on, then finally strutted out. The creep in short-shorts giggled and reached out to hold his hand, but he pushed her aside.

"Tell them," he shouted up to the parapet, "that the Dragon will see the reporter."

As someone went to open the gate the girl guarding us stepped closer and I saw her finger tighten around the trigger of her gun. My flesh went cold. If the police stormed the fort, most of us would die.

The gate opened and I caught sight of someone holding a white flag. Then a tiny woman with red hair came out of the shadows into the fort, staring at the terrorists. Someone from the world outside! It was as though she'd come from another planet.

The Dragon was standing in the middle of the yard, hands on his hips. "You wish to see me?"

"Yes!" the reporter said cheerfully. "And I've brought you something." She walked up to the Dragon and held out a small object. "This is a CB radio sent in by the police. Would you speak to them on it?"

"Absolutely not."

"But why? They want to know your demands so they can begin negotiating."

"The police can wait." The Dragon studied her. "Do you want an interview? Where's your tape recorder?"

The reporter shrugged. "I'll just talk to you, then tell my listeners what you've said."

"How stupid. People want to hear my voice, not yours."

"But . . ."

"Get out of here. Tell your friends in the police that next time I will speak only on television."

The reporter looked our way. "Those poor children. Can't you free them, and keep the adults?"

The Dragon grabbed her shoulders and shook her so fiercely that I thought her neck would snap. "Get out of here!" he screamed, then gave her a shove that sent her stumbling toward the gate. For a moment I was afraid she would try to argue with him, but instead she left without looking back.

When the gate was locked the Dragon began fiddling with the CB radio. Suddenly he ripped something out of it, crushing it under his heel, and threw the radio into a corner of the yard.

"The police tried to trick me," he shouted at us. "That radio was bugged, so it would secretly broadcast my voice from Regimental Headquarters whenever I spoke to my soldiers. The police thought they could trick the Dragon, but they are fools!"

He turned to the woman in short-shorts. "What is your name?"

"Cody."

"Are you prepared to die, Cody?"

She smiled. "I know you don't mean that."

The Dragon removed the pistol from his belt. "Come here."

I gasped and covered my mouth. The smile left Cody's face and she was walking hesitantly toward the Dragon when Kingsley ran across the yard and stepped between them.

"Leave this woman alone," he said to the Dragon. "Pick on a man for a change."

I was so scared for Kingsley that I couldn't watch. There was a long silence, during which I heard Aunt Melody's harsh breathing beside me, and then the Dragon laughed.

"I wasn't planning to harm this woman, just testing her nerves. But don't cross me again."

There was more silence, and I prayed Kingsley wouldn't

say anything else. Finally I managed to raise my eyes and saw Kingsley returning our way. Cody was walking beside the Dragon toward the Regimental Headquarters, laughing and chatting as though nothing had happened. She sure did have nerve, but I still hated her.

"You should have stayed out of it!" I said to Kingsley. "She's a total creep. You could have been killed because of her."

He ignored me and sat down heavily on a bench. "I think that guy is a coward. But, like any coward, he loves to show off by pushing around weaker people. I was ready to hit him, and I think that's why he backed down."

"It was very brave of you to tangle with him," Aunt Melody said.

"You were wonderful, Kingsley!" As I said this, I saw a red glow spread under his tan. He was actually embarrassed, but I couldn't understand why. For several moments Kingsley stared at the ground, then he looked up.

"I have a confession to make. I've been lying to both of you. I . . . I'm not a movie star."

I guess my jaw bounced off the ground, I was that surprised, but Aunt Melody just nodded.

"Why didn't you tell us the truth?" she said quietly.

"I suppose a lie starts small, then it just grows. When I first came to Hollywood, people back home expected to hear big things about me. I couldn't get any work as an actor, but how could I write my foks that I was driving a cab? So I said I was a stage actor in a play. Then when I finally got a tiny part in a film, I pretended it was a really important role. Pretty soon I was lying about everything."

"Why tell us the truth?"

"I don't know for sure, Liz, but when I was facing the Dragon just now, I expected a bullet at any second. I don't want to die a liar."

"So you're only a cab driver?"

"No, I also work in a factory, which is why my hands are calloused." He smiled. "I know you're disappointed, Liz. It's a funny thing, but when you saw me in my taxi last night, I was terribly embarrassed. Now I just want to straighten out my life and be totally honest."

"So you don't act?"

"Yes, I do. But I only have small roles, like in that film I was doing near Minneapolis. When we get out of this fort I'm going to study acting and work my way to the top. No more hoping my looks will get me there."

"Tell me." Aunt Melody said, "Why did you phone me the other night and ask all those questions about my singing?"

"To be honest, when I first met you I thought you could help my career. I figured you might know some people in Hollywood . . . . I'm sorry I tried to use you, Melody."

Don't ask for my thoughts as Kingsley said all this. At first I was disappointed, but I quickly cheered up. After all, I figured it wouldn't be long before Kingsley made it big, and then I could tell everyone I knew him when he was a nobody.

Aunt Melody squeezed Kingsley's hand and they smiled at each other. Boing! My heart went pitty-pat, and I was mentally trying out the sound of "Uncle Kingsley" when I saw the Dragon coming our way. At his side was the Creep, also known as Cody.

"All kids stand up!" the Dragon shouted. "Hurry!"

What now? I hated that man, yet I was so frightened of him that I leapt to my feet and waited in a cold sweat for his next order. I was so scared of dying that I would have done anything to get out of that fort.

"You," the Dragon said, pointing at Serena. "Step forward."

For a moment Serena didn't move, and there was a cheeky look in her eyes that worried me. If she challenged the Dragon, she'd be the loser. Just as I was about to say something, she walked forward.

"Yeah?"

"What's your favourite Disneyland food?"

"The Matterhorn Sundae."

The Dragon smiled. "Sounds good." He turned to another girl and learned her favourite food. Then a little Chinese boy was asked, and two other kids.

"Listen, everyone," the Dragon said. "We're all getting hungry and I know you're tired of the canteen food, so I'm going to order in everything these kids have described and we'll have a big feed. How does that sound?"

The Dragon waited for a response. Maybe he expected cheers or something, I don't know, but he only heard silence until the littlest kid of the group said, "I like it!"

The Dragon laughed and Cody picked up the kid in her arms. "Aren't you a sweetheart!" she said in a sticky-sweet voice that made me want to spew. "How would you like to eat in the Regimental Headquarters with me and the commander?"

The kid's mother gasped, but her husband kept her quiet. The kid disappeared with Cody and the Dragon, and I tried not to let myself worry about him. Instead I watched as a terrorist climbed up to the parapet and, leaning over the logs in the glow of red spot lights, shouted to the police about the food.

Not much later I was tucking into a Matterhorn Sundae. Even though a guard was standing practically on top of me with her gun, and I could see others patrolling the parapets, I still felt incredibly hungry. Was that sundae ever good! Five flavours of ice cream, five toppings, and ringed with a cloud of whipped cream. What a feast, and I made it last because I didn't want to think about the guns.

As I was swallowing the last of the sundae, feeling like my tummy was about to explode, an argument broke out. My throat went tight, and I looked anxiously at Señor Hernandez who had shouted angrily at one of the terrorists. He was really young, but there was something so old about his eyes. They looked tired and they were full of hate. He said something in Spanish, then switched to English as he gestured at our group of hostages.

"I will speak in words these people know, so they will understand how you rich have bled our country dry," he said to Señor Hernandez in a low, tense voice. "You have left us nothing but the cockroaches and the mud. My baby brother is covered with lice and his stomach is swollen from starvation. But look at *you*! Silk shirts, steaks to eat, trips to Disneyland. Do you call that fair?"

"I have come to America to find industries that will invest in our country. They will bring us jobs so your brother will have work when he grows up."

"But he will have no education. The nearest school is beyond the mountains, a day's journey on foot. So what good are the *yanqui* jobs?"

"Without them, La Luceña will always be poor. Give the government a chance to make changes. Please!"

The man lifted his submachine gun and pointed it at Señor Hernandez. "It is too late."

I grabbed Aunt Melody's hand and held it tight. I wanted to scream, or squeeze my eyes shut and block out this nightmare, but I could only stare at the terrorist. *Someone stop him!*

There was a shout from the Regimental Headquarters where the Dragon stood in the doorway. "What are you doing?" he said. "Lower that gun!"

As the terrorist hesitated, my eyes crept down to his trigger finger. The skin was white with tension.

"Lower that gun." The Dragon started walking across the yard slowly and steadily, his eyes on the terrorist. "It's not time for killing yet. When it is, I'll give the order. You are my soldier. Lower your gun."

At last the terrorist obeyed. What a relief! I was just beginning to relax when Señor Hernandez grabbed the Dragon's arm.

"Why have you done this?" he demanded. "What do you want? Why won't you talk to the police? When will you let us go?"

The Dragon shook free of Señor Hernandez's hand. "Perhaps you will *never* leave, sir, except in a wooden box. It makes me sick to think of the suffering your government has caused the people of La Luceña."

"You have no right to talk. You, who calls himself the Dragon, are not from my country. You are only a bandit who hires himself to people like these poor teenagers. What do you care about their cause?"

"I am a freedom fighter. My cause is the liberation of oppressed people throughout the world."

"Empty words! You don't care about the people of La Luceña, so why are you here?"

As the Dragon's cold blue eyes stared at Señor Hernandez, the terrorist spoke. "Without the Dragon we would never have had this success. At last people throughout the world are talking about our cause! They will demand that you help the poor. Give us schools and hospitals. Give us hope!"

"Schools cost money, my friend. Coffee is the only thing La Luceña can sell to the world, and the price has fallen. Meanwhile La Luceña must buy all its oil and that price has risen like a skyrocket. We spend all our money on oil to keep our few tiny industries operating. How can we pay for more schools?"

A look of utter despair appeared in the young man's eyes. "There *must* be a way."

"I have spent seventeen years in the government, searching for a solution to our country's problems. And how did your guerillas thank me? By killing my wife and daughter with a bomb."

The terrorist's eyes dropped.

"Now I see you at Disneyland with your guns, threatening to kill more children." Señor Hernandez reached out his hand and gently squeezed the teenager's shoulder. "Release your hostages. No one has died, and you will be given fair treatment in the courts."

The boy turned his head and I saw that he was crying. "My brother," he whispered. "Must he starve?"

"If you die here at Disneyland, you cannot help your brother. Young people like you can make our country strong, but not with violence."

As the teenager continued to cry, I looked at the other terrorists standing nearby. For that brief moment I wasn't afraid anymore, because I saw in their eyes how much they cared for the boy who was crying. I hoped that they would listen to Señor Hernandez, but then the Dragon broke the spell.

"Your words are very smooth," he sneered. "But it's too late for words. Your government must produce action now, or every person in this fort will die."

"Including these young terrorists?"

"If necessary."

"What good will that do?"

"They'll be martyrs! The people of La Luceña will rise up in memory of their young lives, and drive out your corrupt government."

"I see," Señor Hernandez said, nodding. "And what about you? I notice that you don't include yourself among the martyrs. Are you not prepared to die for the cause?"

The Dragon's hand flashed out viciously, striking Señor Hernandez with a sharp sound. His head snapped to one side, but he remained standing and looked scornfully at the Dragon.

"I thought so. What fools your followers are."

The Dragon turned and walked angrily toward the Regimental Headquarters. Serena went to hug her father, and fear crept back into my heart as I looked at the terrorists' faces. Once again they looked like robots, ready to kill if the order was given.

7

Far above in the night sky I saw the winking lights of a plane, and thought of the people all safe inside. They were probably reading magazines and eating snacks, relaxed and comfortable as they travelled home without a worry in the world. I had to smile, realizing that even flying looked good to me now.

Our little group of hostages was together beside the log wall of the fort. Some of the kids were asleep cuddled against their parents, but the adults were wide awake. I was pleased to see people talking to Mrs. Spencer, the woman from England, but minutes later I watched angrily as Cody returned from the Regimental Headquarters and plopped herself down among us, bold as anything.

"She should go sit somewhere else," I whispered to Aunt Melody. "The way she plays up to the Dragon makes me *sick*."

"She's trying to stay alive, Liz. I'm sure she's very upset, and probably lonely. Why don't you go talk to her?"

"No way! Are you crazy?"

She patted my hand. "Then I'll go. Someone has to be her friend."

My eyes just about yo-yoed out of my head as I watched Aunt Melody sit beside Cody. I felt betrayed.

Crawling over beside Serena, I asked how she was doing.

"Lousy," she pouted. "My whole holiday is spoiled. It's one thing for these stupid terrorists to fight the government in La Luceña, but imagine coming all the way to Disneyland to take hostages."

"They seem pretty desperate. I felt sorry for that guy when he was arguing with your father."

"I can't sleep. Let's go for a walk."

I started to protest, but Serena scrambled to her feet and I followed along. Maybe I thought I had to protect her, or maybe I was just drawn by her strong personality.

Serena said something in Spanish to our guard, who nodded. "I told her we're going to the washroom," Serena explained, "but let's go up on the parapet."

"Are you nuts? They'll shoot us."

"We couldn't escape from up there, and nobody's going to shoot without an order from the Dragon."

Just past the washroom was a blockhouse containing wooden stairs leading up to the parapets. We started cautiously up the steps, and I was so tense that my heart really was in my mouth. It was pitch-black inside the blockhouse and totally silent, so it was a real relief to reach the top of the stairs and tiptoe out onto the parapet.

The red glow of the spotlights blinded me for a moment. As I blinked, trying to get used to the light, I was jabbed in the back by something hard.

"Keep calm," a voice said. "I don't want to kill you."

I almost screamed, then managed to strangle the sound. I raised my hands instinctively, then the gun was removed from my back and the voice told me to turn around.

I lowered my hands and turned to see the boy who had argued with Señor Hernandez. His face was a copper colour in the spotlight's glow, and I could see from his eyes how scared he was.

"Why are you here?" he said, aiming his submachine gun at me, then sliding it over to face Serena.

"Put that thing down," Serena said. "We're not trying to escape. If we climbed over this wall and jumped, we'd kill ourselves. Don't you know that?"

"Then why are you here?"

"We came to talk to you."

We did? I looked at Serena in surprise, but she was smiling at the terrorist as if she really wanted to talk. Suddenly I was afraid she might have some secret plan, a hare-brained escape plot that would get us both killed. I wished I hadn't come with her, but it was too late now.

"Tell me about yourself," Serena said to the terrorist. "What is your name?" She spoke in English, I guess so I wouldn't feel left out.

"My name is Mateo."

"Are you scared, Mateo?"

"Yes, I am very frightened. Look over there." He pointed over the wall, and my heart jumped. Across the river the police had set up powerful spotlights, and in their glare I could see dozens of officers ready to attack. They all held weapons and wore riot gear.

"What's going to happen?" I said, my voice trembling.

Mateo shook his head. "I don't know. They have been lined up there for an hour, and I am so afraid."

"Then why did you come here?" Serena asked. "Didn't you know you might die?"

"Yes, but I did not expect to be so frightened."

"Why don't you surrender?"

"Because the Dragon would not allow it. He gives the orders and it is my duty to obey."

"*Why*?" Serena said scornfully. "The Dragon is not from our country. He doesn't care what happens to our people."

"He must care, or he would not be facing this danger with us."

"Are you paying him to lead you?"

"Of course not. The Dragon doesn't care about money. He is fighting imperialism, to free the oppressed people of the world."

"That sounds really fancy," Serena said sarcastically. "What does it mean?"

Mateo turned and looked toward the darkness to the south. For a long minute he was silent. "When people are oppressed," he said at last, "it means lice crawl in their hair. It means they search through garbage for something to eat. It means they sleep on a dirt floor without even a blanket."

"I don't believe you," Serena said. "Nobody in La Luceña lives like that."

Mateo shook his head. "Your father has kept you from learning the truth, so I'm sure you won't believe there are thousands of children who live in the streets without a home of any kind."

"Where are their parents?"

"Dead."

"Why?"

Mateo sighed. "They have been killed in the fighting between the guerrillas and the government. My parents were shot last year, so I am raising my brother alone."

"Then why are you *here*?" Serena said angrily. "How can you possibly help your brother by being shot dead when the police storm the fort?"

"Someone must do this. I am ready to sacrifice my life if it means the people of La Luceña can be happier."

Serena stared at him. "What about your little brother? What will happen to him?"

"I hope that someone will care for him."

"If not, will he end up living in the streets? Sleeping in doorways and begging for food?"

Mateo nodded.

"But that's not *fair*. Little kids should have a home!"

Mateo smiled. "You sound like one of us. Why don't you take up a gun and fight with us?"

"No." Serena looked at the riot police across the river. "Soon you will die, Mateo. It makes me feel very sad."

All three of us were silent, gazing at those figures with their horrible weapons. My nerves were rubbed so raw that I felt tears running down my face. I brushed them away and put my hand on Serena's arm.

"We'd better go."

She nodded, then looked at Mateo. "At first I didn't believe what you said, Mateo, but now I realize you must be telling the truth. Otherwise you wouldn't be here. I'm sorry."

With his eyes on Serena, Mateo put down his gun. Untying a cord from around his neck, he held it out to Serena. Dangling from the cord was a wooden cross.

"This is for my brother. If I die, will you take it to him? I will tell you how to get to our village."

Serena hesitated, then shook her head. "No."

I looked at Mateo. His eyes were shadowed, but I knew what he must be feeling. "Why not?" he asked.

"Because I don't want you to die, Mateo. It isn't right! Put down your gun and surrender to the police."

Mateo turned toward the waiting police. *"Vaya con Dios,"* he said quietly.

Serena shook her head and walked quickly toward the

blockhouse. I tried to think of something to say to Mateo, then I followed Serena. Neither of us spoke until we were crossing the fort's yard.

"What were those Spanish words he said?"

"Go with God." Serena stopped walking and looked at me. "Why is this happening, Liz? Why is there poverty in my country, and hatred? Why do people have to fight each other?"

"I don't know, Serena."

As Serena stared at me, I knew she was thinking about what Mateo had said. "I want to help my country, Liz. I want to *do* something."

"Maybe things aren't so bad in La Luceña," I suggested, though I didn't really believe it. "Maybe Mateo was making it up."

She shook her head. "Whenever I've asked my father about the fighting he hasn't given me a straight answer. I guess I never really cared until now but when Mateo tried to give me that cross it just . . ."

I thought Serena was about to cry, but instead she turned and walked quickly toward the group of hostages huddled against the wall. Reaching her father, she knelt down and said something that made him frown.

I watched them for a moment, then went to sit with Aunt Melody. After I'd told her about Mateo, I mentioned the riot police waiting across the river.

"Will they attack soon, Aunt Melody?"

She put her arm around me. "Probably not, Liz. Right now they're just trying to frighten the terrorists to try to make them give up. It sounds like Mateo is ready to quit, but I don't think the Dragon would break very easily."

"So the police definitely won't raid the fort tonight?"

"I don't know. But if they do, there will probably be bright lights and a lot of noise. I want you to drop to the ground and lie absolutely still. If the police break into the fort do exactly what they say."

"I'm so scared, Aunt Melody. When is this going to end?"

"Nothing will happen until we find out what the Dragon wants."

"What do you think he wants? Money?"

"Maybe, but if they only wanted money, they could have grabbed any of the tourists here. They went to a lot of trouble to capture Serena and her father, so they must be planning to put pressure somehow on the government of La Luceña."

"To do what?"

"I don't know, Liz. Perhaps in the morning the Dragon will tell the police what he wants, and then something can happen. In the meantime, we'll just have to wait."

The night was so long, and I had such horrible dreams. We all lay huddled together on the ground beside the wall. I never realized before how difficult it is to sleep on a hard surface, and I must have woken up about a hundred times. Finally I opened my eyes to a pale red glow in the sky, and the Dragon standing over me.

"Stand up," he ordered.

At first I didn't move because I was still half in a dream. Then the Dragon kicked me with his boot and the pain made me scramble to my feet.

"What do you want?" I said, trying to sound brave.

"Come with me."

I turned to Aunt Melody for help, but she was sound asleep. Then I looked around for Kingsley, but the Dragon grabbed my arm and dragged me across the yard. I tried to fight him, then I remembered Aunt Melody saying that hostages who fought back were the ones chosen for execution, so I stopped struggling.

We went into Regimental Headquarters where I saw a sub-machine gun leaning against a wall. A terrorist came out of the shadows with a piece of yellow nylon rope. She and the

Dragon tied my wrists behind my back, then hung some heavy packages over my shoulders and blindfolded me. When the Dragon ordered me to start walking my legs wouldn't move.

"I can't," I whispered. "I'm too scared. Please don't kill me."

"Show some courage," the Dragon said angrily. "If you don't, all of your friends will die."

"What are you doing to me? What's in those packages?"

"Plastic explosives. If they go off, there'll be nothing left of you to bury. So start cooperating, little girl."

A hand shoved me from behind. For a terrible moment I felt myself falling, then somehow I found my balance and stumbled forward. The musty smell of the Regimental Head-quarters was left behind and I felt the dirt of the fort's yard under my feet. From the distance I heard Aunt Melody call to me.

"Be brave, Liz! Do exactly as they say."

Again the hand shoved me, and a gun was pushed into my back as I stumbled blindly across the yard. A moment later I heard a rusty squeal, and I knew the gate had been opened. Voices approached. "What have you done to this girl?" a man said angrily. "What are you, some kind of animal?"

"Be quiet, cop, and listen," the Dragon said.

"There'll be no talk until you release this girl."

"You are in no position to make demands. If you want, I'll shoot the girl right now in front of your eyes. Then maybe you police will cooperate."

My knees started to collapse, then a hand reached out to steady me. There was a long silence, during which I made gasping sounds as I fought to keep from fainting. Then the man finally spoke.

"What are your demands?"

"First, ten million dollars in gold. Second, the manifesto of the liberation army is to be read on radio and TV in La

Luceña. Third, the political prisoners on this list are to be released from prison in La Luceña and flown out of the country."

"Is that all?"

"Yes. My demands are simple, but you must do everything by tonight, or I'll begin killing."

"*By tonight?* That's impossible."

"Do as I say, or one hostage will die every thirty minutes."

"Be reasonable. The people on this list must be in prisons all over La Luceña. How could the authorities bring them all together in a few hours and fly them out?"

"That's not my problem."

For the first time another voice spoke and I realized it was Cody. "You cops better listen to the Dragon. He means business."

"Aren't you one of the hostages?"

"Sure I am, but that hasn't stopped me from getting to know the Dragon. The man is clever, and he's brought you cops to your knees. So get working on his demands, or people are going to die."

The Dragon laughed. "You see, even the hostages support me! I don't enjoy killing, but I'll do it if necessary. I am the liberator of the oppressed!"

He was so pleased with himself that he was just about crowing, and I silently swore at Cody for making him feel so good. Nothing more was said by the police officer and, after the gate had closed behind him, I was released from the explosives and the rope.

When the blindfold was gone I blinked in the sunshine and then ran to Aunt Melody. After sobbing against her for a while, I wiped my eyes and saw Kingsley watching me with a worried face.

"Are you going to be okay, Liz? They threatened to shoot anyone who tried to go to you."

I managed to smile. "I guess I'll survive, but it was awful.

When they took off the blindfold I was so glad to be free, but then I realized we're all still trapped. What can we do, Kingsley?"

"Pray. Nothing else will help us now.".

It was a terrible day. I spent a lot of time staring into space — I would daydream about my family, pretending I was home with them, or else I would pray. I knew this experience couldn't end without something terrible happening, but I didn't want to think what it might be.

Occasionally I saw Mateo patrolling the parapets, and I remembered the cross he wanted Serena to take to his little brother. If I could have thought of a way to reach La Luceña, I would have volunteered to take the cross there.

About the only good thing that happened all day was the talk Serena had with her father. Señor Hernandez had admitted that he'd shielded Serena from the truth about La Luceña, but he was really shocked when Serena told him what she planned.

I didn't understand their conversation, of course, but Serena told me about it afterwards. Her whole attitude had been changed by her talk with Mateo, and now she wanted to work with the poor in the villages of her country.

Her father had argued against the idea, saying it was too dangerous, but Serena had dismissed this with a snap of her fingers. I'd never met anyone so strong minded, and obviously she just ran right over Señor Hernandez's objections.

"I feel so happy, Liz! At last I've found something I can do with my life."

It was none of my business, so I didn't say anything more. I just crossed my fingers that it would work out.

A few minutes later the Dragon marched across the yard and motioned for the hostages to be silent.

"All of the children, come here. And make it fast!"

A few parents protested weakly but no one wanted to cross him. Pretty soon our small group of kids was being led toward a corner blockhouse by the Dragon, with Cody at his side, while a guard came behind us carrying a gun.

A little girl looked up at me. "Where are they taking us?"

I shrugged. "How would I know?" But right away I felt guilty for being off-hand. As we started climbing the stairs inside the blockhouse, I reached for the girl's hand.

She looked up with a smile. "My mom says we're going home today."

Her face was so sweet, and there was such trust in her eyes, that I was overcome with hatred for the Dragon. How could he do this to these kids? I looked at him waiting for us at the top of the stairs, and I wanted to tear the smirk off his face with my bare hands.

But I didn't. Instead I leaned close to the little girl. "Promise me you'll do whatever you're told by these people. If guns start shooting, lie down and don't move."

"I promise," she said, squeezing my hand. "I want to go home, you know. I don't want to die."

The Dragon motioned impatiently for us to hurry, then we were herded out onto the parapet. The log wall was too high for the little kids to see over, but my heart thumped when I looked across the river at the blue helmets and grim faces and weapons ready to attack.

"Listen to me," the Dragon said. "Do you kids want to leave here today?"

"Yes!" a boy said, and the rest of us nodded.

"If you don't, it will be the police's fault. If any of you get killed, it will be the police's fault. If . . ."

"Liar!" the boy said. "You're the one who did this, and you make me sick!"

Cody grabbed the boy's shoulders and shook him hard. "Be quiet, kid! If you don't shut up, you'll die."

The boy started to say something more, then Cody shook him again and tears rolled down his cheeks. "That's better," Cody said. "Now button your lip good and tight."

The Dragon looked at the rest of us. "Do you want to live?" When a few heads nodded, he pointed across the river. "You'd better tell the police how you feel. Your fate is in their hands."

"What do you mean?" Serena said.

"You big kids, lift up the little ones in your arms. When I give the signal, start yelling to the police *we want to live.*' Don't stop until I tell you."

I bent down for the little girl and felt her warm arms hug my neck. "We'll do exactly what he says," I whispered, then waited for the Dragon's signal.

"Now!" he shouted.

Only a few little squeaks rose up around me, and I realized someone had to set an example. "We want to live!" I called, then really shouted, "WE WANT TO LIVE!"

The little girl in my arms giggled, then joined in. So did the other kids, loud now, and I could see the police across the river beginning to react. Heads turned our way, officers motioned for quiet, and a man quickly climbed up to the top of a parked van with something which he aimed at us.

For a second I felt faint, then I realized he was holding a mobile TV camera. As we continued to shout, I made out the words KTLA-TV on the side of the van, and I realized the Dragon was getting the world-wide publicity that he wanted.

"That's enough!" the Dragon said. "Good work, kids. I'll send out for some more treats as a reward. Just tell me what you want."

"I'll tell you what we want," Serena replied angrily, putting down the boy she'd been holding. "We want to see you in prison. The sooner the better."

"Yeah!" another kid said, then shut up fast when Cody raised a threatening hand.

The Dragon gave Serena such a dirty look that every kid

on the parapet went absolutely silent. For a moment nobody spoke, then the Dragon's lip curled in a sneer.

"You're the consul's daughter, the one with all the money. What is it like having money that's stolen from the peasants of La Luceña?"

"Are you calling my father a thief?"

The Dragon just smiled.

I put my hand on Serena's arm. "Take it easy. Don't let him get to you."

But I don't think Serena even heard me, she was staring so hard at the Dragon. Then, without warning, she clenched both her fists and ran straight toward him. Probably the Dragon would have tossed her off the parapet, but fortunately Cody grabbed Serena and held her until she stopped struggling, all the while saying, "easy, easy, easy," like she was soothing a runaway horse.

Finally Serena calmed down, but her eyes never left the Dragon's smiling face. "You won't get away with calling my father a thief. He's a great man, and he cares about the people of our country. *You* don't! You're just something that crawled out from under a rock."

"Be careful, or you'll die."

"You keep saying we're going to die, but you never do anything. You're just a fake. You're gutless!"

The Dragon pointed his finger at Serena. "Tonight your life ends." Then he turned and walked quickly away. Cody ran after him, and I looked at Serena.

"You're crazy, Serena. Everyone knows not to talk back to a terrorist, let alone call one gutless."

Serena's breath was coming in short, sharp gasps and I saw that the anger had drained away from her face. In its place was raw fear. I put my arms around her. "Serena, you've got to control your temper. Promise me you won't say another word to the Dragon, or any of them."

"I promise," she said in a weak voice. "Sometimes I just

blow my top, and I do crazy things. . . . He called my father a thief."

"Your dad's not a thief, Serena. Anyone can tell that. The Dragon has a screw loose somewhere. Just calm down, and maybe we'll be out of here before long."

We walked along the parapet toward the blockhouse, arms around each other just like when we met at Castle Dracula. I glanced at Serena and wondered if she could keep her temper under control.

Somehow, though, I knew that would be impossible.

8

The end came quickly.

Shortly after nightfall I was suddenly grabbed by a couple of terrorists. They blindfolded me again, then put the packages of explosives over my shoulders and marched me into the yard. Even though I knew this time what was happening, sweat ran down my body as I felt those explosives bumping against me.

Within minutes the same police officer was inside the fort, negotiating the Dragon's demands. The manifesto had already been read on radio and TV, but the officer said it was impossible to get all the prisoners out of La Luceña so quickly.

"Give us time. We'll have them out by tomorrow night."

"Is the gold ready?" the Dragon asked.

"Yes."

"Then I will drop my demand about the prisoners."

There was a gasp behind me, then a woman said, "But this is wrong! My father is one of those prisoners. You promised he would be set free."

"Be patient," the Dragon replied. "Ten million dollars in gold will buy guns and ammunition. Then we can destroy the prisons and free everyone!"

"But my father. You said he would fly to safety *today*."

"These things take time. We can't expect to achieve everything at once, but here at Disneyland we have won a great victory for the oppressed of the world. Let's be happy with that!"

The woman started to say something more but the police officer interrupted. "When will you release the hostages?"

"I want three helicopters, each with a single pilot. They will fly us all, plus some hostages, to the Los Angeles airport. Have a jet waiting there to take us out of the country."

"And the gold?"

"Place half of it on the jet and the other half in a helicopter. I want the helicopter carrying the gold to be the first to land in the fort, so I can see the gold with my own eyes. There is no way you can trick the Dragon."

An hour later I watched as Mateo and another terrorist chopped down the fort's flagpole so there would be room in the yard for the helicopters to land. I hoped that this nightmare would soon be over, even though I wondered which hostages would be chosen for the escape to the airport. Not me, I prayed, not when I've already had to stand blindfolded in the yard with those plastic explosives dangling from my shoulders.

When the flagpole had been dragged to a corner of the yard, Mateo approached our group of hostages. "The end is close," he said to Serena. "I will ask a final time that you take this cross to my brother if I die."

Serena held out her hand for the cross. "I will pray for you, Mateo. You have given your life for nothing."

"But look what we have gained! The world speaks of nothing but our cause."

Señor Hernandez looked up from his place against the wall. "A month from now you will be forgotten. You have gained nothing."

"But the money!" Mateo said triumphantly. "Ten million dollars. That will buy us weapons, and one day it will build schools and hospitals!"

Señor Hernandez shook his head sadly. "You have a lot to learn, Mateo. I too will pray for you, and our country."

Serena put her arms around Mateo. *"Vaya con Dios,"* she said softly.

There was a shout from the direction of Regimental Headquarters, and then I saw the Dragon striding angrily our way. "What are you doing?" he spat at Mateo. "Don't you know these people are the enemy? Before we came here I warned each one of you not to become friendly with the hostages. Now look at you, with your arms around this girl — the consul's daughter!"

Mateo stepped back from Serena. "I am sorry."

"That's not good enough!" The Dragon paused, staring at Mateo. "I order you to execute this girl."

With a cry of anger, Kingsley leapt at the Dragon. For a moment they struggled, then a terrorist ran forward and struck Kingsley with the butt of his gun. The blow was so savage that Kingsley went down without making a sound and lay sprawled on the ground. Aunt Melody tried to go to him but the terrorist stopped her.

At the same time Señor Hernandez was struggling to his feet. He took one step toward the Dragon, then was shoved roughly backward by a terrorist.

"You animal!" Señor Hernandez shouted. "In the name of God, how dare you threaten a child? If you must kill someone to prove your so-called bravery, then shoot me."

The Dragon smiled. "The girl chose herself for execution when she insulted me. Pray for her soul, Consul."

"I beg you! Shoot me instead!"

Turning his back on Señor Hernandez, the Dragon ordered Mateo to take Serena to Regimental Headquarters to be shot. What happened next was like something in a dream. Nobody spoke as Mateo motioned for Serena to get moving. Tossing her hair, she ignored him and spoke to Señor Hernandez in Spanish. At the words he began crying, and then suddenly Serena lost her courage. Her eyes filled with tears, and I heard her whimper as Mateo grabbed her arm.

He gave her a rough shove in the direction of Regimental Headquarters, and she stumbled away. My own legs were like jelly, and I slumped down on a bench. My breath came in short gasps as I watched Serena pass under a spotlight on the far side of the yard, followed closely by Mateo. When they had entered Regimental Headquarters I couldn't watch any more, and looked up at the Dragon.

He was standing beside us with his hands on his hips, a smirk on his face as he waited for the shots. My heart was thundering inside my chest, and sweat poured down my face as the seconds passed. Surely somebody would stop Mateo!

Suddenly a burst of gunfire erupted from Regimental Headquarters. I'll never forget that sound, not until the day I die. It was a series of explosions, each one shaking my own body as I covered my mouth to keep from screaming. Tears poured down my cheeks and people all around started groaning and crying. No one could believe this was possible.

"Cody," the Dragon ordered, "Tell Mateo I want him up on the parapets. Quickly! The police may attack."

Cody ran off. Within a minute she was back, looking really pale.

The Dragon studied her. "Did you give Mateo my orders?"

She nodded.

"Well, what's wrong then?"

"That girl. I ... I've never seen anyone dead before."

The Dragon laughed. At the same time, Señor Hernandez's sobs became terrible. I think I would have fainted from the horror of what was happening if I hadn't been distracted by the *whoop-whoop* of a siren above us.

The Dragon looked up, startled, then reached for his gun as the siren came closer. I remembered Aunt Melody saying there would be bright lights and loud noises if a police attack came, and I watched as a helicopter came out of the night with the siren sounding from its belly. A spotlight shone brightly from the nose of the helicopter as it slowly dropped toward the ground with dust billowing everywhere.

Every nerve in my body tingled as I waited for the gates of the fort to crash in under a police assault. Several terrorists holding guns stood close to our group of hostages, their eyes jumping between us and the helicopter.

Even the Dragon looked nervous as he approached the helicopter, leaning into the windstorm created by the whirling blades while he kept his pistol aimed at the dim figure of the pilot inside. Opening the helicopter door, the Dragon climbed inside and was lost from sight.

For a moment I relaxed a bit, but then I thought about Serena. No longer caring if the terrorists shot me, I went to kneel beside Aunt Melody who was comforting Kingsley as he slowly regained consciousness.

"Poor Serena," I sobbed. "I just can't believe it. I'm going to get the Dragon if it's the last thing I do."

"Don't try anything foolish. That's why Serena died, and I don't want to lose you."

"I hate him, Aunt Melody! He's not even human."

She nodded. "That's why we must be very careful. This is the end, one way or the other, and we'll only get out alive if we don't take chances."

"What's he doing in the helicopter?"

"Checking the gold, I suppose. After that, if all goes well, he'll lift off in that helicopter and we'll never see him again."

"But what if . . ."

Then I stopped speaking because the Dragon had climbed out of the helicopter. The blood pounded in my veins as he ran our way across the yard and stopped directly above me.

"You!" he shouted, pointing his finger in my face. "On your feet!"

"No," I whispered, shaking my head. "Please, not me. I've already . . ."

"Get up or I'll shoot you and pick someone else."

Aunt Melody hugged me. "Don't argue, sweetheart."

Feeling totally numb, I walked toward the helicopter beside the Dragon. The wind from the big blades was terrible, whipping the radio aerial on the helicopter's nose and forcing me to fight against the blasting air. The pilot was waiting at the passenger door and he helped me climb inside.

"Just stay calm," he said. "Do exactly what you're told."

It almost made me mad, hearing that advice yet again, but I just nodded and tried to smile.

"Fasten your safety belt," he said as I sat down next to a window. Through the plexiglass I could see the fort's walls shining under the spotlights and, in the distance, the huddled group of hostages. Suddenly one of them ran forward, bending into the wind. It was Cody.

"What is it?" the Dragon said, as Cody reached the helicopter.

"Take me with you."

"What?"

"I want to go with you."

"But why? In a few minutes you'll be free."

"I can't explain it . . . but my life has changed since I met you. Everything used to be so . . . *boring*. I've never met a man like you . . ."

The Dragon hesitated.

"Please!" Cody pleaded. "I don't care about the danger. Just let me come with you."

"Climb in."

Cody dropped into the seat beside me and the Dragon went forward to sit beside the pilot. "Okay," he said, putting his pistol against the pilot's head, "Let's get out of here."

"What about Mateo and the others?" Cody asked.

"Two more choppers will land after us," the pilot said. "Our orders are to fly you all to Los Angeles Airport. The rest of the gold is waiting there in the jet."

"What about this girl? Surely we're not taking her out of the country. I don't want a kid tagging along."

The Dragon smiled. "Don't worry, Cody. This kid has a short future."

Before I could react to this the pilot flicked a switch and the fort's yard was swept by the yellow beam of a powerful light mounted on the helicopter's roof. Then the roar of the engine grew louder as the helicopter tilted forward and slowly rose off the ground. As it did, the machine twisted to the left and my view changed. For a brief moment I looked in the door of Regimental Headquarters and saw, in the glare of the sweeping yellow light, Serena lying face down on the floor.

"Oh, no," I moaned.

Cody squeezed my hand. I was so shaken that for a moment I held onto her, then I shoved her hand away. The helicopter rose into the sky and angled away toward the lights of the city. I had a brief glimpse of the Matterhorn, pale white against the night sky, and then Disneyland was left behind.

"Turn off your radio," the Dragon said to the pilot.

"But I need to communicate with the airport!"

"Do exactly as I say, or I'll use this gun."

The pilot switched off the radio. "Now what? I can't land at the airport without some kind of radio contact."

"Turn off all your outside lights. Then change your course and fly straight south."

"But the airport is northwest!"

"Stop arguing and do what I tell you."

The helicopter veered to the left. Below us were thousands and thousands of sparkling lights cut by freeways streaming with traffic. We passed over a drive-in theatre, low enough to see the faces on the screen, and I was amazed that life was continuing as normal. How could people go to a movie when hostages were being threatened so close by?

"Reduce your speed," the Dragon ordered.

"It's very dangerous flying without my running lights. Besides, the other two helicopters won't know where we've gone. They'll fly straight to the airport."

"Into an ambush?"

The pilot shrugged. "How would I know?"

"You'd know because you're a cop. Don't think I'm stupid. At this moment I'm flying to safety with five million dollars in gold. Does that make me a fool?"

The pilot lifted his shoulders slightly.

"Answer me!"

"Okay, I admit you're not a fool."

The Dragon twisted around and pointed that ugly pistol at my face. "What do you think of me, kid?"

I tried to answer but my voice was frozen by sheer terror as I looked into the black barrel of the gun.

"I . . . I . . ."

Cody leaned forward in her seat. "I think you're fabulous, and so does this kid, but she's just too scared to say anything."

The Dragon grunted and turned to stare out the front of the helicopter. "Slower," he said, after reading the compass and ordering the pilot to change course. "I'm looking for something."

"Where are we going?" Cody asked.

There was no reply.

"What about Mateo and the others? If there's an ambush at the airport, have they got a secret plan to escape?"

"No, they haven't. Probably they'll all be killed, but that's the price of fighting imperialism. The people of La Luceña will honour their names."

"What about the five million we're escaping with? What's it for?"

"I'll use it to continue the struggle for the oppressed of the world."

"But how? What will you do with it?"

"Don't worry, Cody, I'll think of something."

It was then I realized that the Dragon had sacrificed Mateo and the others so he could get his hands on five million dollars. I wondered what other revolutions he'd betrayed without anyone ever knowing the truth.

"There!" the Dragon exclaimed. "Bring the helicopter down in that football field."

The helicopter hovered for a moment, then began to descend into darkness. I saw a scoreboard with a neon sign reading OUR LADY OF THE ANGELS HIGH SCHOOL, and the dark outline of a classroom block. Directly below us the field was completely black except for a bright path made by the headlights of a parked vehicle.

"Land beside that beam of light," the Dragon ordered, "but not in it. I don't want anyone to see us."

"Someone may hear the chopper," Cody said.

"The houses and roads aren't close enough. No one could tell exactly where we're coming down. We're safe as long as no one sees us."

There was a soft thump when we touched the ground, and

immediately the headlights outside were turned off. Moments later a van came out of the darkness, swung around, and backed up to stop at the rear of the helicopter.

"Oh, no!" the Dragon exclaimed, pointing in the opposite direction.

The pilot turned to look and the Dragon struck him viciously with the pistol. Then he opened the pilot's door, shoved him out, and turned to Cody.

"We've got to work fast. Help us unload the gold."

"What about this kid?"

The Dragon grabbed the helicopter's first-aid kit, took out a bandage and tossed it to Cody. "Tie her hands with this, then come help with the gold."

As soon as he'd climbed out of the helicopter I looked at Cody. "Please don't let him kill me. Please!"

"Listen, kid, just sit still and be quiet. That's the only way you'll live through this."

"But . . ."

"Shut up!"

I said nothing more as Cody began to wrap the bandage around my wrists. Then I remembered my dad describing how he'd escaped once when a man had tied him up. As Cody wound the bandage around my wrists, I pushed out on them just like Dad had done. When she was finished and had hurriedly climbed out of the helicopter, I relaxed my wrists.

The bandage was loose.

A door opened behind me and I turned to look. A stranger, who must have been the driver of the van, reached in to grab one of the square containers stacked in the rear of the helicopter. Staggering under the weight, he carried the container to the van and heaved it inside.

Cody carried a container to the van and then the Dragon took one. First, though, he put down his pistol beside the door so he could have both hands free to work. I knew I'd been given a chance.

I had to escape before the Dragon picked up that pistol again. If I didn't, I was convinced he would shoot me as soon as they were ready to escape.

Turning to face forward so the Dragon wouldn't know what I was doing, I wiggled my hands back and forth inside the bandage and finally managed to slip out of it. Sweat was running into my eyes, but I didn't dare wipe it away. The only sounds I heard were grunts and the occasional muttered swear word, until suddenly there was a loud crash followed by a thump.

"You fool!" the Dragon said. "That container almost landed on my foot."

"I'm sorry," Cody replied. "It slipped. These things are so heavy."

"Pick it up, and hurry. We've got to get out of here."

There was a moment of silence, then Cody said, "It's so heavy! I'm wrecking my back."

"I'll get it."

Shifting in my seat, I saw the Dragon and Cody both bending toward the ground. *Now!* I whispered to myself. Popping open my seat belt I scrambled across to the helicopter door and dropped to the ground.

As I landed, pain tore through my ankle. I tried to run, but my ankle gave out and I fell, almost landing on the unconscious pilot's body. At the same time a voice shouted from the other side of the helicopter.

"That kid's gone!"

The Dragon swore. "I should have killed her when we landed. You two keep loading the gold. I'll go find her."

Moaning with fear, I crawled away into the darkness. The only light came from inside the helicopter, a yellow glow that spread out from the windows and seemed to fill every hiding place as I stumbled forward on my hands and knees, barely noticing the pain in my ankle.

Terrified by not being able to see the Dragon, I turned to look behind me. I had crawled a fair distance from the helicopter so that each window was now just a small yellow shape. But one of those shapes was blocked by the black outline of the Dragon coming my way.

A tiny whimper escaped from my mouth as I lay down on the ground and drew my arms and legs tight against my body. Shivering with horror, I watched the Dragon come closer and closer, then stop.

For a moment he remained motionless, then his dark shape disappeared into the night. I took a deep breath, trying to control my shaking, and listened for sounds that would tell me where he had gone.

Finally, when I'd heard nothing and couldn't stand the tension anymore, I rolled over and sat up. The Dragon came out of the darkness, his white teeth glistening as he smiled.

"On your feet," he said. "You won't waste my time ever again."

Reaching down, he gripped my shoulder and yanked me up from the ground. Then he dragged me toward the helicopter, ignoring my cries of pain as I stumbled along on my injured ankle.

Passing the pilot's body, we went around the helicopter toward the cargo door where the Dragon had left his pistol. It was missing, and so were Cody and the other man.

"What . . . ?" the Dragon said.

There was a muffled sound and we both looked into the rear of the van. The other man lay on his back, his hands tied and a gag in his mouth. He tried to say something, then rolled his eyes and motioned with his head.

Neither of us had a chance to make sense of what he was trying to say, because at that moment Cody stepped out of the darkness holding the pistol. "I'm a police officer," she said quietly to the Dragon. "You're under arrest."

9

If you think I was shocked, you should have seen the Dragon.
His eyes bugged and his jaw dropped to somewhere around
his knees. "Who?" he finally managed to say. "What?"

"Lift those hands," Cody said, motioning with the pistol.
"Fast!"

By the time the Dragon's hands were up, his cool was back.
He even managed to find a smile, and he flashed it at Cody.
"Good work, girl. You fooled me completely, but I still want
you with me. Let's take off with the gold. This kid can stay
here, and so can my partner."

"Where would we go?"

"Into hiding, while I sell the gold. Then we'll travel to
anywhere you want. Paris, Monaco, Rio, you name it."

"Who will you sell the gold to?"

"Tell you later. Now put down that pistol and let's get moving."

Cody hesitated, and for a terrible moment I thought the Dragon had won her over. Then she shook her head. "I was hoping you'd identify your connections for selling the gold, but that can wait until you reach police headquarters."

The Dragon took a step toward Cody, but she waved him back. "No tricks! On the ground, spread eagle."

When the Dragon was flat on his face, Cody told me how to get help on the helicopter radio. It was really exciting to break the news to the police about the capture, but then I remembered Serena, and choked up. Even worse, I wondered what had happened to Aunt Melody and the others.

Minutes later sirens and about a million flashing lights came out of the night and raced toward us across the football field. What a sight! The cars skidded to a stop and officers jumped out all over the place waving guns. Cody kept the Dragon covered until he'd been handcuffed and taken away by a small army of officers. Then she turned to me with a smile.

"Liz, I apologize for everything that happened. I didn't dare let the Dragon suspect who I really was."

"I don't mind, Cody! That was the biggest shock of my life, when you came out of the shadows with the gun. Up to that minute I hated you."

She nodded. "I think everyone at the fort did, except your aunt. Not that I blame them, but it felt pretty lonely."

"Everyone thought you'd gone over to the Dragon's side. I guess it's lucky he thought so, too."

"I wanted to keep an eye out for the kids, and I was also hoping the police could use me in some way. They knew I was inside because that was my own commanding officer who came into the fort when you were blindfolded, but I guess they couldn't come up with a plan."

"Why were you at the fort?"

She smiled. "It was my day off so I was visiting Disneyland with my boyfriend. He was one of the people who were released at the beginning."

"You took a big risk, talking your way onto the helicopter."

Cody shrugged. "I had to protect you, and of course I was anxious to nail the Dragon. Police all over the world have been after him for years, but I got him!"

She grinned and gave me a big hug. An officer slapped Cody on the back, then someone else shook her hand, and all the while I kept wondering about Aunt Melody. My chance to find out came after medics had taped my ankle and revived the helicopter pilot who was taken away in an ambulance. As someone else got into the helicopter to fly it away, I turned to Cody.

"Could the helicopter take me back to Disneyland so I can find out if Aunt Melody is okay?"

Cody nodded and a few minutes later I was looking down at the red and blue patterns of flashing police lights as we lifted away from the football field. Beside me Cody was neatly rolling the bandage she'd used to bind my wrists.

"I've never been so tense," she said, putting it back in the first-aid kit. "After I tied you up I had to figure a way to capture both the Dragon and the other guy. That's why I dropped the gold, hoping to break the Dragon's foot so I could grab the gun. When that didn't work, I was planning to take a chance and go for the gun anyway. That's when you made your break."

"Did you know I'd flexed my wrists so the bandage would be loose?"

Cody nodded. "I figured you might get away. When you did and the Dragon went after you, it gave me a chance to arrest the other guy. But there was no way I could find the Dragon out there in the dark."

"Cody, I was so scared."

She laughed. "Me too, Liz, but now it's all over."

"Except for Aunt Melody and the others. I wish I knew what's happened to them."

The pilot looked back. "Two hostages were taken with the other terrorists when they escaped to the airport. They went straight into an ambush."

"What ambush?"

"The jet was a special one with secret roof panels. When the terrorists walked into it the panels opened and a police SWAT team jumped down on them. Every terrorist was arrested, with not a shot fired."

"So the hostages got out safely?"

"Yup. It's a happy ending for everyone."

Except Serena, I thought. It was horrible to realize that we'd all be going home safely, but poor Señor Hernandez would leave Disneyland without Serena, his only family.

"Have the other hostages left Disneyland?" Cody asked.

"Not yet. Medics are still in the fort checking them out, and they're also being questioned by some officers."

"Are we going to land inside the fort?"

He shook his head. "Too many people running around in there. I think I'll just drop us down at New Orleans Square."

All of Disneyland was lit up as we slowly descended out of the night sky. Every building on Main Street U.S.A. was outlined in white bulbs, and Sleeping Beauty's Castle was pink and a delicate blue. The pilot said that normally Disneyland is open at night, but the whole place had been closed to the public since the hostage-taking began, so I only saw police officers as the helicopter touched down.

The decks of the stern-wheeler *Mark Twain* were circled by creamy white bulbs glowing in the darkness. Beyond it, fireflies twinkled in the trees, and Big Thunder Mountain shone red against the sky. I was really safe at last.

"I can't wait to see Aunt Melody! Where do you think she is?"

"The hostages are coming across from the island now. Let's go to the pier."

A large group had gathered by the river, staring in the direction of Tom Sawyer Island. Some of them looked like friends and relatives of the hostages, while others were obviously reporters. Every eye and every camera was aimed at a boat coming across the river with a load of hostages wrapped in blankets.

Aunt Melody wasn't among them, but I still pushed close to watch the boat land. Flash cameras were going off constantly and the TV lights made the hostages look unreal as they came ashore. Most of them were crying or shaking their heads.

"I'm safe!" the grandmother from England said as she was grabbed by a young man and hugged until I thought her bones would break. Another hostage threw away his blanket and did a little dance while the TV cameras followed him. Then he suddenly threw up his hands, laughing hysterically.

"We actually got out alive!"

As I watched him, someone grabbed me from behind and I turned to see Señora Garcia.

"You're safe!" she exlaimed. "Your aunt's been frantic with worry."

"Where is she, Señora?"

"Coming from the island. I'm so glad you're alive! My little Ramón is safe, too. He's at police headquarters."

"In a cell?" I said, then smiled. "I didn't mean that, Señora Garcia. He's a super kid."

What a lie, I thought, but it didn't hurt to be nice after all she'd been through. I was just about to ask how Señor Hernandez was feeling when I saw a boat land with Aunt Melody, and I ran to hug her.

After we'd clung to each other, tears splashing all over the place, I described everything that had happened at the football field. I'd just finished my story when Kingsley appeared, and I had to repeat the whole thing.

A final boatload of hostages landed and I saw Señor Hernandez hobble ashore. Breaking away from Aunt Melody and Kingsley, I went toward him with a pounding heart, trying to think of something to say. But I never got the words out, because suddenly a dark figure raced off the boat and gave me the most enormous bear hug.

It was Serena.

At first I just held her, wanting to be sure she wasn't a mirage, and then I stared into her smiling dark eyes.

"How . . . What . . . ?"

"It was Mateo! When we got to Regimental Headquarters he said he couldn't shoot me. He made me promise I'd lie face-down on the floor until every terrorist was gone from the fort, then he fired his gun into the wall. It scared me so much, Liz, just hearing that gun and knowing how close I'd come."

"I almost forgot, Serena! The Dragon's been captured, and guess who arrested him? Cody!"

"What? Impossible!"

Well, did we ever have a great time, both of us talking at the same time about what had happened. I thought nothing could improve on that night, but I was wrong.

As Serena and I babbled away, I looked toward the river bank and saw, in the shadows of a tree, Kingsley and Aunt Melody leaning close to each other, talking very intently. For a minute I waited for the Big Kiss, but then I realized something more important was happening between them.

It's called friendship, the kind that lasts forever.

About the Author

Eric Wilson was born in Ottawa and now lives in British Columbia. He is often "on the road" visiting schools to speak about his writing, or exploring various regions of Canada to discover settings for future books.

His earlier mysteries are described on the following pages, and you can also learn how to get your membership in the exciting Eric Wilson Mystery Club.

Have you joined

THE ERIC WILSON MYSTERY CLUB

?????

It's exciting, and it's all FREE!

Here's what you'll receive:
— a membership card
— a regular newsletter
— a chance to win books personally
   autographed to you by Eric Wilson

It's FREE, so just send your name, age,
address and postal code to:

The Eric Wilson Mystery Club
Collins Publishers
100 Lesmill Road
Don Mills, Ontario
M3B 2T5

MURDER
ON *THE CANADIAN*

A Tom Austen Mystery

Eric Wilson

As the train's whistle moaned out of the black night, Tom fell into an unhappy sleep. It was broken by a scream.

The agonizing sound of a woman's scream hurls Tom Austen into the middle of a murder plot on board the sleek passenger train, *The Canadian*. Who is responsible for the death of lovely Catherine Saks? As Tom investigates the strange collection of travellers who share Car 165, he gets closer and closer to the truth . . . and then, without warning, he is suddenly face-to-face with the killer, and his own life is threatened in the most alarming possible way.

"In MURDER ON THE CANADIAN there is excitement from the start; the first dozen pages produce a bomb, a "deadly enemy", a drunk and a beautiful woman . . . there are plenty of suspects to lay false trails, and the action moves as fast as the train."

Times Literary Supplement

VANCOUVER NIGHTMARE
A Tom Austen Mystery
Eric Wilson

Tom's body was shaking. Spider could return at any moment, and there was still a closet to search. Was it worth the risk? He hesitated, picturing Spider bursting through the door with rage on his face.

A chance meeting with a drug pusher named Spider takes Tom Austen into the grim streets of Vancouver's Skid Road, where he poses as a runaway while searching for information to help the police smash a gang which is cynically hooking young kids on drugs.

Suddenly unmasked as a police agent, Tom is trapped in the nightmarish underworld of Vancouver as the gang closes in, determined to get rid of the young meddler at any cost.

" *'The coffin was open, the air black and musty all around.' Who could resist a mystery begun in such a fashion? This fast-paced tale of drug smuggling and deceit will be an instant success...*"
Canadian Book Review Annual

THE GHOST OF LUNENBURG MANOR
A Tom & Liz Austen Mystery
Eric Wilson

"Would you like to visit a haunted house?"

With this invitation from a man named Professor Zinck, Tom Austen and his sister Liz are swept up in spine-chilling events that will baffle you, and grip you in suspense.

A fire burning on the sea . . . icy fingers in the night . . . an Irish Setter that suddenly won't go near its master's bedroom . . . a host of strange characters with names like Black Dog, Henneyberry and Roger Eliot-Stanton . . . these are the ingredients of a mystery that challenges you to enter the ancient hallways of Lunenburg Manor . . . *if you dare.*

"Eric Wilson has once again produced an excellent, fast-paced mystery . . . the richness of the Maritime setting—replete with phantoms, folklore, stormy seas and superstitions—enhances the story."
The Ottawa Citizen

THE KOOTENAY KIDNAPPER

A Tom Austen Mystery

Eric Wilson

Only groans and creaks sounded from the old building as it waited for Tom to discover its secret. With a rapidly-beating heart, he approached the staircase...

What is the secret lurking in the ruins of the lonely ghost town in the mountains of British Columbia? Solving this mystery is only one of the challenges facing Tom Austen after he arrives in B.C. with his sidekick, Dietmar Oban, and learns that a young girl has disappeared without a trace. Then a boy is kidnapped, and electrifying events quickly carry Tom to a breathtaking climax deep underground in Cody Caves, where it is forever night...

VAMPIRES OF OTTAWA
A Liz Austen Mystery
Eric Wilson

Suddenly the vampire rose up from behind a tombstone and fled, looking like an enormous bat with his black cape streaming behind in the moonlight.

Within the walls of a gloomy estate known as Blackwater, Liz Austen discovers the strange world of Baron Nicolai Zaba, a man who lives in constant fear. What is the secret of the ancient chapel's underground vault? Why are the words *In Evil Memory* scrawled on a wall? Who secretly threatens the Baron? All the answers lie within these pages but be warned: *reading this book will make your blood run cold.*

SUMMER OF DISCOVERY
Eric Wilson

Rico's teeth were chattering so loudly that everyone could hear. Ian's breath came in deep gasps. A gust of wind slammed through the old building, shaking it so hard that every shutter rattled, and then they heard the terrible sound. Somewhere upstairs, a voice was sobbing.

Do ghosts of hymn-singing children haunt a cluster of abandoned buildings on the Saskatchewan prairie? The story of how the kids from Terry Fox Cabin answer that question will thrill you from page one of this exciting book. Eric Wilson, author of many fast-moving mysteries, presents here a tale of adventure, humour and the triumph of the human spirit. It's an experience you'll never forget.